Bofuri ★ I Don't Want to Max

MAPLE

Maple's STATS

Lv29	HP 1,3
MP 22/22	
[STR 0]	[VIT 1,
[AGI 0]	[DEX 0
[INT 0]	

Skills

Martyr's Devotion
Indomitable Guar
Bomb Eater, Gian
Taunt, Deflect, Ins
Sidestep, Great S
Cover, HP Boost (S

Welcome to
NewWorld Onli

"Full Deploy—Commence Assault!"

The skill the bygone deity
had bestowed upon her.

Innumerable weapons came into
being, so black that they seemed
hewn from the darkest night sky.

In the Graveyard of Dreams

"Maple, thank you so much!
We gained so many levels!"

"I'm sure we can help out now!"

Adorable clothing—a pleasing mismatch with the dual hammers of destruction.

Outside the Maple Tree Guild Home

Skills

Martyr's Devotion, Fortress, Absolute Defense
Indomitable Guardian, Psychokinesis, Hydra Eater,
Bomb Eater, Giant Killing, Atrocity, Meditation
Taunt, Deflect, Inspire, Shield Attack,
Sidestep, Great Shield Mastery IV, Cover Move I
Cover, HP Boost (S), MP Boost (S)

MAPLE'S STATS

Maple

Lv.29   HP 1,300/1,300
MP 22/22
[STR 0]   [VIT 1,080]
[AGI 0]   [DEX 0]
[INT 0]

Bofuri
★ I Don't ★
Want to Get
Hurt, so I'll
③ Max Out My
Defense.

YUUMIKAN

Illustration by **KOIN**

YEN ON
NEW YORK

Welcome to
NewWorld Online.

YUUMIKAN

Translation by Andrew Cunningham • Cover art by KOIN

ITAINO WA IYA NANODE BOGYORYOKU NI KYOKUFURI SHITAITO OMOIMASU. Vol. 3
©Yuumikan, Koin 2018
First published in Japan in 2018 by KADOKAWA CORPORATION, Tokyo.
English translation rights arranged with KADOKAWA CORPORATION, Tokyo, through TUTTLE-MORI AGENCY, INC., Tokyo.

Yen On
150 West 30th Street, 19th Floor
New York, NY 10001

Visit us at yenpress.com • facebook.com/yenpress • twitter.com/yenpress
yenpress.tumblr.com • instagram.com/yenpress

First Yen On Edition: September 2021

Yen On is an imprint of Yen Press, LLC.
The Yen On name and logo are trademarks of Yen Press, LLC.

Library of Congress Cataloging-in-Publication Data
Names: Yuumikan, author. I Koin, illustrator. I Cunningham, Andrew, 1979– translator.
Title: Bofuri, I don't want to get hurt, so I'll max out my defense / Yuumikan ; illustration by Koin ;
    translated by Andrew Cunningham.
Other titles: Itai no wa Iya nano de bōgyoryoku ni kyokufuri shitai to omoimasu. English
Description: First Yen On edition. I New York : Yen On, 2021–
Identifiers: LCCN 2020055872 I ISBN 9781975322731 (v. 1 ; trade paperback) I
    ISBN 9781975323547 (v. 2 ; trade paperback) I ISBN 9781975323561 (v. 3 ; trade paperback)
Subjects: LCSH: Video gamers—Fiction. I Virtual reality—Fiction. I GSAFD: Science fiction.
Classification: LCC PL874.I46 I8313 2021 I DDC 895.63/6—dc23
LC record available at https://lccn.loc.gov/2020055872

ISBNs: 978-1-9753-2356-1 (paperback)
       978-1-9753-2357-8 (ebook)

10 9 8 7 6 5 4 3 2 1

LSC-C

Printed in the United States of America

I Don't Want to Get Hurt,
so I'll Max Out My Defense.

NewWorld Online Status

NAME Maple | LV **29**

HP 200/200 MP 22/22

STATUS

STR 000 VIT 321 AGI 000 DEX 000 INT 000

EQUIPMENT

New Moon: Hydra | Night's Facsimile: Devour | Black Rose Armor

Bonding Bridge | Toughness Ring | Life Ring

SKILLS

Shield Attack | Sidestep | Deflect | Meditation | Taunt | Inspire | HP Boost (S) | MP Boost (S)

Great Shield Mastery IV | Cover Move I | Cover | Absolute Defense | Moral Turpitude | Giant Killing

Hydra Eater | Bomb Eater | Indomitable Guardian | Psychokinesis | Fortress

---

NewWorld Online Status

NAME Sally | LV **24**

HP 32/32 MP 80/80

STATUS

STR 055 VIT 000 AGI 153 DEX 045 INT 050

EQUIPMENT

Deep Sea Dagger | Seabed Dagger

Surface Scarf: Mirage | Oceanic Coat: Oceanic

Oceanic Clothes | Black Boots | Bonding Bridge

SKILLS

Slash | Double Slash | Gale Slash | Defense Break | Inspire | Down Attack | Power Attack

Switch Attack | Fire Ball | Water Ball | Wind Cutter | Cyclone Cutter | Sand Cutter | Dark Ball

Water Wall | Wind Wall | Refresh | MP Cost Down (S) | Heal | Affliction III | Strength Boost (S)

Combo Boost (S) | Martial Arts V | MP Boost (S) | Magic Mastery II | MP Recovery Speed Boost (S)

Poison Resist (S) | Gathering Speed Boost (S) | Dagger Mastery II | Fire Magic I | Water Magic II

Wind Magic III | Earth Magic I | Dark Magic I | Light Magic II | Combo Blade II | Presence Block II

Presence Detect II | Sneaky Steps I | Leap III | Fishing | Swimming X | Diving X

Cooking I | Ancient Ocean | Chaser Blade | Superspeed | Jack of All Trades

Defense Build and a Series of Blunders

Kaede had started *NewWorld Online* only because Risa asked her to. But her extreme defense build had made her character, Maple, so tanky that she'd ranked third in the first event and earned herself plenty of in-game fame.

The day before, the game's second event had taken place. She'd joined in, playing alongside Risa's character, Sally. Maple's defense had carried the day again—they'd reached their goal of ten silver medals each, and she'd exchanged those for two new powerful skills.

The morning after…

Kaede sat up in bed.

"I didn't sleep much…"

According to her internal clock, it felt like a full week had come and gone since she'd slept in that bed. It was harder than expected to drift off like usual.

Rubbing her eyes, she rolled out of bed, got ready, and headed to school.

"It's gonna be a scorcher…"

She moved as quickly as she could without breaking a sweat.

*   *   *

When she got to class, Risa was already there.

The two of them always arrived early, so they had the classroom to themselves.

"Mornin', Kaede."

"Mornin', Risa!"

Kaede dumped her things on her desk and then went over to where Risa sat.

"Feels like it's been ages since we last came to school!"

"Right? I mean, we did spend seven days in-game... Which reminds me, Kaede. You'll need to be careful today."

"Huh? Of what?"

Kaede couldn't think of anything particularly concerning.

"In-game, we've always gotta be on the lookout for monsters or hostile players. There's a risk you'll bring that habit into the real world."

Risa explained how easy it would be for Maple's and Sally's routines to spill over into their regular, everyday lives.

"I've been playing awhile, though. Nothing like that's happened before."

"Yeah, it's more of a 'just in case.' This is the first time you've been logged in for a full week, right?"

"True... All right! I'll be careful."

As they spoke, more classmates started arriving.

Five minutes before class started, the pair wrapped up their conversation, and Kaede headed back to her own desk.

After school...

Kaede staggered into her room and immediately buried her face in her pillow, screaming.

"Today never happened!"

However, her memories told a different story.

*   *   *

First bell…

"*Zzz…zzz…*"

Because of her restless night, Kaede was nodding off in class. Something she *never* did.

Her seat was close to the windows and often bathed in sunlight. This proved to be her undoing.

Moreover, people who don't normally fall asleep in class are all the more likely to suddenly wake up.

(Incidentally, everyone had long since recognized Risa as someone who could nap through anything.)

At the teacher's prompting, the girl next to Kaede gave her a poke.

"Mm…mm? *Yawn…* Is it my turn to keep watch? …Huh?"

Stretching as she spoke, she heard her voice echo in the classroom.

And everyone turned to stare.

By the time Kaede realized where she was, it was too late.

"I warned you," Risa whispered.

"Try to pay attention," the teacher said.

"R-right. Sorry."

That was only the first incident of many.

The next came during the break after third bell on her way back from the bathroom.

The halls were packed with students traveling to their next class.

And a girl walking behind Kaede happened to bump into someone trying to pass by. She dropped her textbook and pencil case.

Both hit the ground with a loud clatter.

"……!"

Kaede immediately spun around, her left hand held high and her right reaching for her waist, the same way she had practiced over and over after Risa taught her how.

If she'd been in-game, this would have been the ideal response.

But here at school, she had neither shield nor short sword.

"Huh? What the…?"

The girl behind her was stunned by Kaede's bizarre pose.

Kaede slowly let her arms fall, smiled awkwardly, and then quickly walked away.

By this point, her nerves were totally frayed.

Two very public blunders would do that to anyone.

Not wanting to screw up again, Kaede tried to keep a close watch on her every move.

But the third time's the charm.

The more you try not to mess up, the more likely it becomes.

After lunch, the class was playing dodgeball in the gym.

Kaede and Risa were on the same team.

That fact alone ensured their victory.

No matter how hard they tried, nobody could ever hit Risa.

Even when their opponents aimed all their shots at her, it wouldn't get them anywhere.

Outside of the VRMMO, there was no compelling reason to pull off risky, last-second evasions, so it was a breeze for Risa to dodge everything.

"She's incredible in this world, too…," Kaede muttered.

Of course, if she hadn't been so caught up watching Risa's performance, she might have avoided her third horrible mistake.

"…Kaede!"

The enemy team had suddenly decided to aim at someone *besides* Risa, hoping they might actually knock out a few people.

The ball was already hurtling toward Kaede...

She was much too focused on Risa to react in time.

When Risa yelled, Kaede looked toward the ball—and saw it coming right at her.

On any other day, she'd have ducked or jumped sideways.

But for the past week, she'd avoided projectiles in a very different manner.

"Cover Mo— Eaugh!"

She caught herself mid-yell and clapped her hands over her mouth...meaning she could neither dodge the ball nor catch it.

And hits to the face still counted.

"Kaede?! You okay?!"

"I'm fine..."

From Kaede's perspective, as long as no one was paying any attention to what she had been about to shout, then she'd live.

The silver lining was that she and Risa were the only ones in class who played *NewWorld Online*, so apparently, nobody recognized the phrase.

"I'm gonna rest over there..."

"Good idea."

Kaede slumped against the wall, her head on her knees.

That was her final lapse in judgment.

"...Maybe I should take a break from the game."

Just to be safe, she decided to not log in at all for three whole days.

Whether because of her ban on gaming or perhaps through sheer force of will, by the third day, Kaede finally stopped having accidents.

CHAPTER 1

Defense Build and New Features

After her self-imposed exile ended, Maple logged in and waited for Sally in the square. It was definitely less packed than the moments leading up to the last event, but there was a *lot* of chatter. Maple looked around, wondering what was going on.

A few minutes later, Sally joined her.

"Sorry, am I late?"

"No, I basically just got here. What's the plan for today?"

"Hmm, well…you've been offline for three days. Have you kept up on the news?"

"News? No, I haven't heard anything. I was trying to keep my distance…"

Had something happened during her break?

Not only had she stayed away from the game, but she'd also avoided any and all media related to it.

"Lemme give you a rundown, then."

"Please."

"First, they've added a new great-shield skill. One that counters piercing damage."

"Ooooh!"

Maple was delighted.

According to Sally, they'd even made the conditions needed to acquire the skill public information.

Maple made a mental note to investigate that later.

"This next bit is the biggest change—while you were out, a new event...or more like an update came out and added new enemies and features."

"Oh yeah?"

"Out in the field, you can catch these golden insects called glowbugs."

Sally explained that there were several types, and if you beat one, it dropped a Glowbug Seal.

"And what do you use those for?"

"The new feature—they're required to buy a Guild Home."

"A what?"

"This town's got lots of places you can't go in, right?"

"Yeah."

Maple glanced around, spotting several.

The town they were standing in was quite large, but most buildings were inaccessible—

The main exceptions were the NPC shops. Players could also pay an NPC to open their own smithies or the like. Everything else, however...

"One seal lets you buy one home. The properties available have different ranks, and which rank you can buy depends on the type of bug you beat. Purchasing a Guild Home provided a reliable home base to operate from on each stratum."

"Aha. Interesting."

There were quite a few other advantages to Guild Homes. There would eventually be Guild Home–exclusive items that provided status-boosting blessings. There was just one catch...

"For now, there's a finite number of glowbugs. Same as the number of available properties."

"Agh, really?!"

"The admins say they'll continue adding properties as time goes on, but…"

But that didn't mean there'd necessarily be more glowbugs.

And Maple was already behind the curve.

"We've gotta find one!"

Maple definitely wanted her own Guild Home.

And if they didn't find a seal quickly, they might never get another chance.

This was no time for talk!

"Maple."

"Wh-what is it?"

Sally opened her menu and took something out of her inventory.

"I already got one. I figured you'd want it."

"Oh…ohhhh! Thank you!"

"But…this just gives us the *chance* to buy a Guild Home. We still need the actual money."

You could form a guild without a Guild Home, but that wouldn't provide the blessing Sally had mentioned.

"How much do we need?"

"The seal I got is the lowest-ranking one, so…five million gold."

"Fi—?! …That's a lot."

Far more than Maple had scraped together to commission White Snow from Iz. It was a genuinely astounding price tag.

Maple hadn't saved more than she needed for the custom shield.

And after daily expenses like potions…she only had maybe fifty thousand gold.

"So…we're grinding for gold today, right? I want a Guild Home soon."

Maple turned to head out of town.

"Maple."

"Y-yes?"

Sally opened her status menu and stepped closer.

She tapped the corner of the screen, showing it to Maple.

The counter for Sally's current funds displayed one five and six zeros.

"I also went ahead and got the money sorted out."

"W-wow! Sally, you're amazing!"

"Heh-heh-heh! Keep the praise coming."

Sally took a moment to bask in Maple's adoration.

She hadn't used any exploits to get this money. She'd simply hunted monsters and sold their drop items for three days straight.

Once they were ready to get down to business, Sally suggested checking out the available homes. Maple nodded vigorously.

Sally had already done some scouting, so she took the lead.

"I'll pay my share later!" Maple promised.

"Hmm… Nah, we're good. I don't really *need* gold. If you gotta make it up to me, just hand over any gear you find that might help me out."

"…Okay! No problem! I'll try to get you something good."

"No rush."

Sally stopped near the edge of town.

The area was rather far from the central square and most NPC shops.

"Around here."

"That was a long walk."

"If we had a higher rank seal, we could get a big Guild Home near the center of town, but…"

"I'm grateful for the one we have!"

Maple wasn't overly concerned about the size or location of their future home.

Given her personality and disposition, this did not come as a surprise.

It didn't take them long to find an available Guild Home. On their way over, Sally had explained that if a property was taken, the crest on the door would vanish.

"Hmm... I could dig it."

The building stood at the end of a deserted street. A small, modestly decorated wooden door sat at the base of a stone staircase.

Out of the way, but not impossible to find—just the right degree of secluded.

"This definitely looks like it's up your alley, Maple."

"Should we?"

"Yeah, why not?"

"Let's do it."

"Okay!"

Maple took out her Glowbug Seal and pressed it to the door.

White light filled the alley, the crest on the entryway lit up, and the door slowly opened.

They stepped inside their Guild Home.

"Ooooh, it's roomier than I expected."

She glanced around the interior and spotted mostly wooden furniture, all soothing, earthy tones.

The back wall had a blue screen built into the wall, and entering info there let the user set guild membership.

Sally ceded the honors, so they made Maple the guild master.

"This is in the lowest tier of Guild Homes, but even that lets us register...up to fifty members."

"There's two floors, but…would that many people fit in here?"

"Well, it is the upper limit, so it probably wouldn't be comfortable. Anyone you wanna invite? We'd better hurry before they join some other guild."

Maple thought about this; then an idea hit her.

"…Oh! What about Kasumi and Kanade?"

During the second event, they'd worked with Kasumi to escape the underground cave in the desert and, by pure luck, had run into her again on the last day. They'd also met Kanade during the same event. Maple had become fast friends with him, and the two had wound up playing Othello on a beach together.

"I figured you'd say that. Go for it."

Maple sent them both a message and both answered a few minutes later.

Fortunately, neither had joined a guild yet.

And they were happy to accept Maple's invite.

"Score! Sally, I'm gonna meet them at the square!"

"Sounds good. See you in a bit!"

Maple flung the door open and ran off.

It wasn't long before she was back at the square.

Kanade and Kasumi were seated on nearby benches. Both got up when they spotted Maple approaching.

Neither had met the other before, so there was a round of introductions.

"Thanks for accepting my invite!" Maple said. "I'm really excited you guys are joining!"

"I'm happy you thought of me."

"You have my thanks."

With that, they turned to go.

And as they did…

"Mm? That's…"

Maple paused after catching sight of someone—who saw her looking and promptly came over.

"Whassup, haven't seen you since the event," he said.

"Chrome! Feels like that was ages ago, but I guess it hasn't been that long."

When Maple first started playing, Chrome had been the one who introduced her to the blacksmith Iz. He was a fellow great shielder and had done quite well for himself in the first event. Maple was all smiles, genuinely pleased to have bumped into one of the few people she knew in the game.

Their last meeting had been on top of a snowy mountain.

"How'd you make out in the last event?" he asked. "You hit up that mountain boss after us, right?"

That mountaintop had been home to a fearsome giant bird.

"It was crazy strong! We barely won."

Chrome had suspected this might be the case, but actually hearing it still came as a shock.

Wow. She actually beat that thing.

His party had gone up against it and had been wiped out almost instantly—proving once again just how strong Maple really was.

"With your strength, you could join any guild you want. Well… some of them have very specific conditions."

"Oh, that reminds me! Would you like to join my guild, Chrome? If you don't have other plans."

Chrome had run the second event with a full party, so Maple had figured he was already in a guild with them.

That was the main reason she hadn't sent him an invite earlier, but since they'd bumped into each other like this, it couldn't hurt to ask.

"Really? If you'll have me, I'm happy to join."

Chrome explained that his event party had been a onetime thing.

In other words, he had no reason to refuse.

The four of them headed to her Guild Home.

"We're back!"

"Welcome... Oh? You brought Chrome, too."

"When we bumped into him, he agreed to join!"

"In that case, let's get you all signed up."

Each of them entered their info on the blue screen. Once that was done, it was time for Maple's speech.

"Uhhh, guess I'll start from the top. I'm Maple, the guild master. I'm very good at defense and poison attacks!"

She bowed low. Everyone else joined in, naming their fortes. Sally's evasion, Chrome's advanced great shield techniques, Kasumi's close combat, and Kanade's ranged magic and balance.

"Just one thing left...the guild needs a name."

"You choose, Maple. You're the guild master, after all."

"Agreed."

"Same here."

All four of them looked at Maple.

She thought about it, then entered a name on the screen.

Maple Tree

They were few in number, but the legend of this newly minted guild was only just beginning.

In time, they'd earn themselves nicknames like Den of Fiends or Hellscape, but that was still to come.

Maple was soaring over a field on Syrup's back. She'd Giganticized the pet she'd acquired during the second event and then climbed aboard her extra-large turtle.

There was no question that this was much faster than her walking speed.

"Kanade! Thanks for coming today."

"You can count on me!"

Kanade was along for the ride to help with resource gathering.

The day after the guild's founding, Iz, the crafter who had made Maple's White Snow, also joined their ranks, and she'd brought all her crafting talents with her.

Maple and Kanade were currently headed for the mines to stock up on supplies for the Maple Tree forge.

Sally, Chrome, and Kasumi were elsewhere, farming monsters for wood and fabric drops.

Iz poured everything into crafting, so no combat for her.

Fighting with next to no combat skills would've been less than ideal.

She more than made up for this in crafting versatility.

Weapons, clothes, accessories—even furniture was possible.

If it could be crafted, she could make it.

"I'll handle security and leave the mining to you!"

"Akashic Records comes in handy here. I was lucky enough to get Mining V from it."

Akashic Records

Grants nine random skills, three each from Crafting, Combat, and Other categories.

> Skill levels are set at (M) or V.
> Skills vanish after one in-game day from activation.
> Does not grant skills already learned.

Kanade had activated Akashic Records earlier, and it just happened to spit out Mining V—so for today, he was a solid miner. That was the only reason he and Maple were the ones headed for the mines.

Armed with a pickax, they were on the hunt for ore.

"Golems usually show up in these mines," Maple said. "Leave those to me!"

"I can only use staves, so even if I pull other weapon skills, they'd be useless. It's pure luck whether I can fight or not on any given day."

Akashic Records would really start to shine once Kanade went up a few more levels and could fight without relying on the skill's random boons.

It could open up all kinds of novel strategies.

After all, Kanade could have a completely different set of skills every twenty-four hours.

This meant the ace up his sleeve was always changing—a downright terrifying concept in PVP. Unpredictability conferred a huge advantage.

"Mines spotted!"

"Woo! Let's do this!"

Syrup had been mistaken for a rare monster on a few occasions, causing spells and arrows to come flying their way, but each time, Maple jumped down in front of the attacking players and scolded them for it.

Naturally, it wasn't so much her admonishment that stopped the attacks as much as it was the sheer shock of having Maple dive-bomb them. Maple herself remained blissfully unaware of this.

"Stay close until we get farther inside."

"Will do!"

They entered the tunnel, heading deeper into the mountain.

There were no pretty crystals like the snail cave, but instead there were exposed veins of ore here and there. Each time they found one, Kanade pulled out his pickax and got to work.

"Onward!"

"I'm with you!"

Maple had put Syrup back in her ring so she could focus on protecting Kanade.

The golems they encountered were easily beaten by her weaker poison attacks, so there was no need to bust out her great shield or Hydra.

She made sure to pick up everything they dropped after each battle.

These mines offered a variety of ores, but rare ones weren't easily found.

"Iron Ore, Gray Crystal, Pebble..."

Kanade's pickax clanged again.

Each hit gave him more materials, but nothing worth writing home about yet.

They followed the forking paths, delving deeper...until they'd finally hit all the gathering points in the mine.

"Well...quantity over quality!" Maple said.

"Still...this was a pretty bad run," Kanade said, frowning.

Quality was actually far more important.

"So how do we get out? If we wander aimlessly, will we find the exit eventually?"

"Actually, I remember the way we came."

"Oh really? You're smart! Then take point, please!"

Kanade led the way through the mine-shaft maze, and they unerringly made it back outside.

Meanwhile, the others were in a forest.

This expedition was geared for combat and hunting monster drops.

"Sally, you're as bad as she is...," Chrome muttered under his breath.

He was watching Sally dodge attacks like a leaf in the wind. A tree monster was flinging roots up from the ground while a wolf was darting around, launching itself at her.

No matter how certain it seemed that they would land a hit on her, Sally always dodged just in the nick of time, and no attacks ever made contact.

"Whoa...this aura is amazing...," Sally muttered.

A halo of bluish-white light enveloped her.

Sally had spent quite some time grinding monster drops for gold—a *lot* of monster drops.

This had boosted her level and granted her a new skill.

Sword Dance

+1% STR each time you dodge an attack.
Max 100%.
Buff vanishes if you take damage.

To earn this skill, you had to reach level 25 without ever taking damage.

Whenever the skill was active, the telltale aura appeared.

There was no way to beat Sally without attacking her, but the more her opponents missed, the more her advantage grew.

"Even with this, I'd still struggle with Maple's tankiness."

"Hmm... Just how high is Maple's VIT exactly?" Kasumi wondered.

"Why not ask her?" Sally said, shooting Chrome a quick glance. "She'd probably tell you."

Chrome's own fighting style was, in a word, steady.

Block cleanly with his great shield, hack away with a short sword.

He handled the shield with practiced ease, deflecting incoming blows with precision. And he always kept an eye on his surroundings, positioning himself so he couldn't be surrounded.

"That's a *normal* great shielder."

"Basically, yeah."

Not as flashy as Maple's usual way of doing things, but his core gaming ability was definitely superior.

Maple had no need to block or defend the way he did, so she didn't make particularly good use of her shield.

Her body was sturdier than any shield, after all.

Most of the time, she was actually keeping the shield out of the way to avoid wasting Devour. That skill could swallow enemies whole and did ludicrous amounts of damage, but it had limited daily uses.

"Normal players are a minority in *this* guild."

Maple's, Sally's, and Kanade's builds were all unorthodox.

Kasumi and Chrome were more conventional.

Iz was a pure crafter, so that alone put her one step removed from the norm.

Once Chrome wrapped up his battle, the three decided to head home.

"Simply being in this guild may mean I won't be 'normal' for much longer," Kasumi mused.

"I was thinking the same thing."

"There's a good chance we all start being more and more like Maple."

Hard to say if that was good or bad.

Once both parties delivered their hauls, it would be Iz's time to shine.

The two groups ran into each other outside of town and continued the rest of the way together.

The five of them in a single group drew numerous stares.

Maple's fame required no explanation. Chrome and Kasumi had both ranked in the first event, and their gear alone drew the eye.

More than a few people reflexively reached for their weapons when they spotted Sally.

As for Kanade, his staff took the shape of a Rubik's Cube that kept coming apart and putting itself back together—just his way of entertaining himself.

It should have come as no surprise that they wound up with a crowd on their heels.

CHAPTER 2

Defense Build and a Quest

The day after the material gathering, Maple was alone in the second-stratum town.

Everyone else was busy with various errands, so she was on her own for the time being.

The second event had kept her so busy, she hadn't gotten any chances to explore the town—this was the perfect chance to do just that.

"I wouldn't wanna force anyone to come along, either."

Besides, it was fun to explore at your own pace.

Her main goal was to find good gear for Sally.

If she could find some skills or gear for herself while she was at it, she'd have no complaints. Maple still didn't have any equipment for her head, so that would be ideal.

Maple started by talking to any NPCs she stumbled upon.

Unfortunately, there were tons of triggers she couldn't activate with her current stats.

Essentially, anything with prerequisites besides VIT was totally inaccessible.

Sally's Superspeed was a good example; Maple could talk to the same NPC, but the quest chain wouldn't start. Since Maple's build was so extreme, even options that were open to most great shielders were off-limits.

"Let's try a little off the beaten path."

The farther away from downtown she went, the thinner the crowds got.

Most buildings she walked by were Guild Homes, and she couldn't enter any of them.

She wandered the back alleys for a while and eventually found several buildings she *could* go in, but they were all abandoned.

"Oh, this one's open, too!" Maple said as she passed through the doorway.

Inside was a single room. A girl was lying on a shabby bed, a woman fretting over her—presumably her mother. There was a small table and two chairs nearby. The china cabinet had the bare minimum place settings—another sign they were not well-off. The girl on the bed kept coughing, looking miserable.

"Hmm? A visitor? Sorry, I didn't see you come in."

"Oh, that's okay."

"There, there," the mother said, her attention already back on her daughter. "I know it hurts."

Uncomfortable, Maple was about to quietly leave, but before she got the chance, the woman turned toward her.

"Um…are you a knight?" she asked.

"Huh? Uh…a-am I?"

Maple's gear certainly resembled that of a knight more than a mage or a run-of-the-mill sword fighter.

"Oh, noble knight! Hear my plea. Please aid my daughter! I can offer no reward, but…please show us mercy."

A blue screen appeared in front of Maple. She read the writing on it.

Quest: The Benevolent Knight

There were two buttons below that—YES and NO.

Maple pushed YES.

No way she could ever hit NO after hearing a request like this.

She didn't care if there wasn't a reward.

"Th-thank you so much! My daughter needs medicine. But I'd never make the journey alone. I can guide you. Will you accompany me?"

"...Got it! I'll protect you!"

Maple rapped her breastplate, and the woman moved closer.

An HP bar appeared above her head. If she didn't keep this woman safe, it would all be over.

The blue screen showed the quest details.

Maple read them carefully, making sure she didn't miss anything.

Her mission was to escort the mother to her destination safely, but there was no time limit.

"Well, for starters, let's make our way out of town," Maple said.

As they started walking, the woman began talking.

"Our destination is the Tree of Life. It's due east."

"Roger that!"

Maple summoned Syrup from her ring, told it to use Giganticize, and then climbed on. It was faster than walking, so she usually traveled this way now.

The woman was clearly programmed to stay within a two-yard radius of the quest-taker, so when Maple climbed aboard Syrup, she put a foot on Syrup's leg, then jumped aboard in a single bound.

"Are we sure you aren't stronger than I am?"

"We should head east."

"Uh, okay… Psychokinesis!"

Like always, she made Syrup rise into the air, and they drifted away.

◆□◆□◆□◆□◆

"I can see the forest up ahead. The entrance is over there."

"Does that mean I can't fly?"

Maple set Syrup down outside the forest, patted its head, and put it back in the ring.

"I'll be counting on your help again later."

She could always summon Syrup if and when she needed it.

Maple scanned the area.

"Come, we should hurry!"

"Got it! Is this…the right place?"

There was a small trail ahead of them.

The woman was pointing at it, so that was probably the way forward.

Maple decided to not wait any longer and set off.

The woman was inside the range of her Cover skill, so she would be easy to protect.

Normally, this quest would have featured a slew of encounters along the way, but Maple had conveniently skipped those, thanks to Syrup.

"Paralyze Shout!"

Maple's attacks couldn't harm the NPC, so even when there were enemies on all sides, her skills made quick work of them.

"I don't even need to kill any!"

However, Maple was much slower than your average player.

That meant she got attacked more often.

By the time they reached the center of the forest, she was out of Devour.

"Hmm… Let's try out the crystal one."

Amethyst Geode was a shield made of purple crystals that Maple had found during the second event. After switching to it, she followed the woman's lead. This particular shield came with a skill called Crystal Wall, which fittingly generated a wall made of crystal on command. Maple drew the natural conclusion that this should help her protect the NPC.

"There! That is the Tree of Life!"

The woman ran over to a tree that was maybe half the size of the trees around it.

"That's…definitely not what I expected," Maple muttered.

She'd been expecting a giant tree bathed in heavenly light.

Maple watched as the NPC got to work. The woman looked over her shoulder, saying, "These help cure sickness."

She plucked several leaves, showing them to Maple.

"Huh… Cool. Can I grab some, too?"

Maple tried, but there was an invisible wall, and she couldn't get close.

Apparently, this was a quest-limited item that players weren't allowed to collect themselves.

"I'm finished."

"Then let's head back! I'll keep you safe!"

Maple called Syrup out again, but this time she had it levitate before making it giant—there wasn't enough room in this forest to follow the usual routine.

"Syrup, pick me up!"

Syrup usually helped her up onto its back (with its mouth), but it was too high up to reach.

Maple thought for a moment how to remedy this, and an idea came to her.

She wouldn't need to climb a tree or jump.

"Crystal Wall!"

Purple crystals spawned directly underfoot, launching her into the air.

Needless to say, this was not the intended use.

"Syrup!"

In midair, Syrup's jaws closed around her torso.

Anyone watching would have undoubtedly been horrified by the sight.

Most would have sworn that she was clearly being eaten alive by a giant flying turtle.

Instead, it tossed her onto its back.

"Oh, what about her…?"

While Maple was busy looking down and searching for the NPC, the woman casually vaulted off a nearby treetop, neatly landing on Syrup's back.

"Holy…!"

"Let's go. My daughter is waiting."

"R-right…"

With that, they flew off once more.

As they did, Maple muttered, "Does she even *need* my help?"

The NPC clearly could have handled this mission solo.

As they came to the forest's edge…

"*Haah…haah…* Thank you for protecting me. I thought I was done for!"

"You're joking, right?! Wh-what are you even saying?"

Maple hadn't done anything special, and Syrup was just flying normally.

She wondered if maybe the flight itself was noteworthy.

If it had been anyone else on this quest, they'd be stuck on the ground, facing powerful monsters, and great shielders generally sacrificed DPS, so most would have been battered around quite a bit.

The woman's line had clearly been scripted to follow up an encounter like that.

It was Maple's unorthodox approach that made the line seem incredibly odd.

"You're a very kindhearted knight."

"Uhhh… I feel like I should apologize or something…"

Maple winced and bowed her head, but the woman ignored it.

This was too awkward to bear, so Maple flew back as fast as she could.

"All right! We're here!"

Maple landed Syrup right outside of town and sent it back to the ring.

All that was left was returning to the woman's house.

"Thank you so much! I'd better hurry home."

She ran off—too fast for Maple to keep up.

"…Guess I'll take my time."

Odds were, the next scene wouldn't happen until Maple got there, so there wasn't much risk of the quest progressing without her. Most great shielders would have been able to match the NPC's pace, though.

Maple made her way to the woman's house. Eventually.

When she opened the door, the woman was in the middle of helping her daughter take a drink of some dark-green liquid.

To Maple's eye, the girl seemed very reluctant—it must have been quite bitter.

Ultimately, the girl swallowed and made a face.

"…How do you feel?"

"*Cough, cough…* Mm. A little better. *Cough! Cough!*"

"But your cough is so bad…! Ahhh! Whatever shall I do?!" the woman wailed.

A screen popped up in front of Maple.

Quest: The Benevolent Knight 2

The next mission in the quest chain.

Maple accepted it right away.

"Oh, generous knight! You will aid me yet again?"

"S-sure. Can't just quit now!"

The kid was coughing a lot. Honestly, it seemed like she'd gotten worse.

"Then please take me to the Spring of Exorcism! It's to the northwest!"

"Right. On it."

The woman immediately started moving toward the edge of town.

"Mm? I picked up a new skill…"

Benevolent Knight

These words had been added to her skill list, but there was no description or indication of what it did.

Just the skill name.

"Uh…does it have no effect? Because the quest isn't over yet?"

In that case, she really couldn't leave things unfinished now. Maple followed the woman.

*　　*　　*

"To the northwest!"

"All righty, northwest it is."

This involved another Syrup flight, which was now simply Maple's default mode of transportation.

As Syrup took to the skies right outside of town, loads of players saw it happen. A chorus of shocked cries went up. Even players who'd heard the rumors gaped at the sight. And Maple's fan club just smiled warmly as they watched her cause yet another uproar.

How quickly the outlandish becomes commonplace.

It would not be long before the entire player base simply reacted with, *Oh, Maple's flying again.*

"This isn't gonna end with two, is it? There's no way there isn't a third part," Maple muttered.

Maple didn't think these things ever came in pairs. It wouldn't feel like enough.

The latest quest wasn't noticeably different from the last one, and that only reinforced her hunch that this wasn't over yet. As she considered how to avoid unnecessary fighting, Maple realized something important.

"Augh! Devour hasn't recovered!"

Fortunately, this dawned on her while she was still aboard Syrup.

It could have been really bad news if she'd only noticed mid-fight.

"Hmm… Well, if the enemy seems too strong, I guess we'll just have to turn back."

There was no point if she let the woman die.

Maple decided she'd better scout the spring from the air, then figure out her plan after that. For now, she followed the NPC's directions.

◆□◆□◆□◆

The spring lay right below Maple's eyes.

This time, the woman didn't say anything, so she'd gone ahead and flown straight to the objective.

The spring in question was nestled inside some craggy outcroppings.

"I guess we should look for a spot nearby to land."

She found a place to set Syrup down, returned it to the ring, then started winding her way to the spring with the woman.

There didn't seem to be any monsters in the area, and they reached the spring without incident. Maple stayed on guard against ambushes, but none materialized. The woman finished gathering water and turned back to Maple.

"Kind knight, I thank you for your help once again!" She bowed low.

"Yeah…I didn't do anything…," Maple commented awkwardly.

"Let's hurry back!"

"Uh, sure. Why not?"

They returned to the landing zone, at which point Maple summoned Syrup again. Then they flew away without incident.

"S-still nothing? Really?"

Maple made it all the way back to town without so much as breaking a sweat.

Like the previous quest, the woman immediately ran off for home to give her daughter the spring water.

While Maple stood there watching.

"How do you feel?"

"I-I'm fine. Don't worry about me," the girl said. But she was very pale and trembling.

She did *not* look fine.

Clearly, they weren't done yet. Maple waited for the next screen to spawn.

Quest: The Benevolent Knight 3

"Yup. Saw that coming."

Predictably, the quest chain continued.

Maple checked the Benevolent Knight skill, but it was still nothing more than a skill name.

Once again, Maple accepted the new quest.

"Oh, noble knight! I am ever so grateful!"

"I've come this far, so I'll make sure to see it through!"

"There is a great city far from here. I've heard of a ring that can heal ails and ills by simply wearing it. I realize that's not much to go on, but can you bring it to me?"

"So...a large town? You mean the one on the first stratum?"

Maple wondered if that was the town she had frequented when she first started playing.

That was the only place that came to mind.

"Could the ring possibly be...?"

She took a ring out of her inventory.

This was a rare drop she'd found early on—the Forest Queen Bee Ring.

"Oh, magnificent knight! You brought the ring? How can I ever thank you?!"

"Wait, this is actually what you were looking for? Seriously?"

Maple hadn't equipped it in a while, so she had no problem handing it over.

It was a rare drop, but not something she could never find again.

Plus, the equipment she was wearing was more than enough; she wouldn't miss it.

"I'll put it right on her..."

The woman took the ring over to the girl and slipped it onto her finger.

Once she did, Maple got the quest-clear notification, proving this had been the right answer.

With the ring on, the girl's cough went away and her complexion improved. Even Maple could tell she was doing better.

"Is she okay now?" Maple asked, relieved.

But a moment later, the girl's face crumpled. She seemed to be in more pain than before. Worried, Maple went over to her.

"Unh...augh. Gah..."

"...What's wrong? Does it hurt anywhere?"

"Augh...!"

The girl let out a hideous groan, then vaulted off the bed, threw open the door, and ran outside.

"W-wait!" her mother called, chasing after her.

As Maple gaped at them, a new screen popped up.

Quest: The Benevolent Knight 4

Obviously, Maple accepted it.

"Right... Guess we're off to the edge of town!"

Maple followed after them, as fast as she was able to.

"There she is!"

She found the woman sitting on the ground outside town.

Maple went over, and the woman started talking.

"Sniff... Oh, noble knight. My daughter...she..."

"Where'd she go? Is she okay?"

"She went to the Temple of Everlasting Darkness... Few places are more dangerous...!"

"...I'll bring her back!"

"Let me guide you there! I can't abandon my daughter!"

Maple would rather go alone, as she wasn't sure she could keep the NPC safe, but it seemed like that wasn't an option, so they left for the temple together.

Maple boarded Syrup and, following the woman's directions, headed northwest past the spring.

There, she found a crumbling old temple. Clearly the Temple of Everlasting Darkness. Maple braced herself.

Keeping one eye on her surroundings, she put Syrup back in the ring before stepping inside.

The temple interior was simple—just a large open space surrounded by walls and topped by a ceiling. A familiar girl lay at the back of the room.

The woman tried to run to her, but before she could, a pitch-black fog started gushing out of her daughter.

As they watched, the fog took on a humanoid shape and solidified—a monster with no face but two sets of large claws. Ignoring the girl, it hurtled toward the woman.

"Cover Move! Cover!"

Maple had made sure to check whether she could use these moves with the NPC on the first leg of the quest.

They allowed her to jump between the woman and the monster and block the attack with her great shield.

*   *   *

"...! I'm out of Devour...!"

Maple had been blowing through these quests so fast, she'd forgotten that she'd long since used up her last Devour for the day.

She still successfully blocked the blow, though, and the monster jumped back.

"I've gotta find a way to use Hydra..."

Clck...kkkkkkkk!

"...This thing is bad news."

Maple inspected her foe. It had no mouth but was making a horrible grinding noise.

Krrrrr...

"Cover!"

Its lunging attacks were straightforward enough that even Maple's unpolished technique could easily block them.

But Maple had limited attack options. She couldn't afford to miss, so timing was critical.

Naturally, that prolonged the battle.

She grimly held her ground until the thing suddenly reared up, clutching its head and screaming.

"GgggrrrraaaaaaaaaaaAAAaaaaAAH!"

Since the shadowy creature had no face, it didn't exactly have expressions per se, but the body language suggested it was in pain.

The monster's arms transformed, merging its claws together into two menacing points—like two lances.

"! Cover!"

When it launched another attack at the woman, Maple instinctively guarded her—but the fused claws were incredibly sharp, and that meant piercing damage.

"Ack... Oof!"

Maple's shield techniques weren't good enough to knock either arm aside.

She lost a good chunk of her HP, but she couldn't stop using Cover now.

The woman clearly wouldn't survive if one of those attacks hit her.

Maple soaked several more attacks from behind her shield, face twisting in pain as she endured the onslaught.

"Gggrrrkkkaaaahhh! Grrrggg…gkkkaaah!"

"Huh…?"

The monster had been attacking nonstop, leaving Maple gritting her teeth against the pain…but it suddenly stopped, backing away. Maple quickly yanked out a potion, keeping an eye on it.

"Gkkkkk…guhhhhh…"

It was clutching its head, curled up on the floor…and then it started to fade. Soon, it vanished completely.

"I—I survived?!"

Maple only had 20 percent health left. She'd been looking for an opening to land a counter in hopes of turning the tables, but the odds had been decidedly against her.

"Finally… The Holy Water of Exorcism must have kicked in," the woman explained.

"You mean…the stuff from the spring?"

"My daughter may have been possessed by a demon."

As the woman said, Maple had won without attacking because she'd successfully cleared The Benevolent Knight 2.

To complete that quest properly, the player had to bring the woman back home without either the player or the NPC dying. If either died, it automatically failed.

But successful or not, the quest chain would advance.

For a great shielder, fighting that battle without clearing the spring quest would be a tall order.

"Oh...the quest just ended."

She'd been trying to figure out what to do next when the message popped up in front of her. Maple blinked at it a few times.

No signs that a new quest was starting, either.

The skill hadn't changed.

"Let's check on my daughter!"

"Oh, right. Good idea!"

They rushed over to the girl and checked her condition.

She was sleeping like the dead. The woman shook her, but there was no response.

"For now...I'd better get her back home."

The woman picked up her daughter and left the temple.

As she did, another screen appeared in front of Maple.

Quest: The Benevolent Knight 5 and Extra Quest: Martyr's Devotion available.

Please choose your route.

"Huh?"

This unexpected twist left Maple baffled.

While Maple was clearing quests, the admins were going about their days like usual—

Until one of them saw something on his screen that made him yelp.

"The Martyr's Devotion quest is active!"

"Wow. Well done. That won't happen unless you keep damage to the mother under a very low threshold. Who...?"

The admin got that far, then cradled his face in his hands.

"Yup. It's Maple… She's, uh…flying."

After hearing that grim pronouncement, the listening admin sighed deeply. He could already see where this was going.

"…Yeah, okay. Nothing we can do about that. It'll be fine. Probably."

"Third stratum comes first."

"Yeah…imagine her flying across those skies. With Martyr's Devotion active, it'll make perfect sense!"

"It's like Fortress turning into Giant Fortress."

"Exactly! Is that an issue?"

"Nope! That should be no problem."

"Good."

"Yep."

""Ha-ha-ha…""

They shared a hollow chuckle that quickly faded into silence.

"This is a disaster!"

"I know! What do we do?!"

Too many players already knew that Maple had become a flying fortress. There was nothing they could do but hold their heads in abject panic.

◆□◆□◆□◆□◆

Maple decided to pick the extra quest and then left the temple, searching for the woman.

There was no sign of her.

"Did she go on ahead?"

She looked around for a bit just to make sure, then hopped on Syrup and headed for the town.

*   *   *

Once she was back, she went to the woman's house.

"…What's going on?"

She quietly opened the door.

The girl appeared to still be sleeping—peacefully. No signs of her earlier suffering.

"Noble knight, my daughter…she isn't waking up."

The woman's voice wavered. Like she couldn't believe this was happening.

As Maple moved closer, she realized the girl wasn't breathing.

"Huh…? N-no! Why?"

"I… I'll go buy an apple for her. She loves apples…"

The mother stood up and staggered toward the door.

Unable to face reality, she was completely beside herself.

"Eh? B-but the quest chain is still active, right?"

Maple hurried to check her quest tab but then noticed a pale glow surrounding the girl's body.

She moved closer until she was standing right next to the bed.

Maple studied the girl, trying to figure out what was going on.

"The light…is writing something?"

The glow emanating from the girl began to coalesce into letters.

"Three days from now…at the Ruined Church?"

When Maple read the message out loud, the glow began to fade.

"I have to go there? But where is it? I don't think there's a place like that around here… Maybe it's outside of town? There *was* a library… I could check there for starters."

By the time the woman came home, Maple was ready to leave.

Maple paid the aforementioned library a visit.

"Let's see… Are there any maps?"

She searched for a book with a map of the second stratum. Her status menu featured a digital map, but that showed only the basic lay of the land, her current location, and the names of some notable landmarks. It certainly didn't have the location of any Ruined Church.

Her search turned up several maps here, but none of them was particularly detailed.

At best, she could roughly make out the terrain.

"Hmm... That's not what I'd hoped for."

But there was plenty of time before the deadline. After deciding she'd played long enough for one session, she put a pin in her investigation.

The following day...

She'd completed her research and emerged from the library.

"Should've known it'd be on the history shelf... I totally missed it..."

Maple had stumbled upon a book about the in-game history, and sure enough, it mentioned a small church.

"Okay, so I still have two days! Right, I dunno what's in store, so I'd better stock up on potions."

Fully prepared, Maple did *not* forget to visit the church at the foretold time. Once again, she was flying there.

"You make this so easy, Syrup!"

She doted on her immensely helpful pet as they flew south. After landing at the edge of a certain forest, she proceeded deeper into the sea of trees.

"It's way less tiring when I don't have to protect anyone..."

Every now and then, monsters would appear and bounce off her armor.

But none of them could damage her.

To Maple, it was like they weren't even there.

But when she didn't have Syrup to ride, her movement speed was ridiculously slow, so it took her a full two hours to walk from the forest entrance to the church.

"Whew... Been a while since I walked that far."

It had been much more taxing than she'd anticipated. Maple wondered if she should explore on foot a little more often.

That said, she eventually reached the run-down church.

"All right! Let's go in!"

The doors were long since gone, and the interior was covered in vines and weeds.

She proceeded down the aisle between the pews.

There was a large cross hanging on the wall ahead—dilapidated, but no less imposing.

Something glittered on the floor below it.

"What's this...?"

It was a little bottle with what seemed like glowing gas trapped inside.

Maple examined the item description.

Archangel's Fragment

"W-wow, that sounds like a big deal."

She carefully placed it in her inventory, scanned the area in case there was anything else of note, and after finding nothing, hurried (as much as she could) back to the girl.

When Maple opened the door, the young girl's mother looked up.

"Kind knight, what brings you here?"

"Something I wanna try."

Maple stood next to the sleeping girl, took the bottle out of her inventory, and opened the lid.

The girl's body began to glow.

"Whoa?!"

"Is something wrong, noble knight?!"

When Maple yelped in surprise, the mother looked baffled.

"Er...can't you see this?"

The glow around the girl shifted—previously, it had formed words, but this time it took the shape of a beautiful woman.

Maple watched closely as the apparition of light began to speak.

"Thank you. I nearly robbed this poor child of her life."

"Oh, wow... Th-that would have been bad..."

"I shall grant you a fraction of my power... This way I, too, can take my leave."

And with that, the light rose up to the ceiling and disappeared.

Once it did, the girl opened her eyes and sat up.

"Huh? Mom?"

"Oh...oh...ohhh!"

The mother threw her arms around the child.

Her daughter seemed mostly confused.

"I guess...all's well that ends well?"

Maple also found this conclusion baffling, but the quest-clear notification popped up, so that appeared to be a wrap.

Outside, Maple checked her new skill.

"Martyr's Devotion... Holy crap! What in the...?"

Maple hastily read the details.

Then she turned and ran toward the Guild Home.

* * *

"Iz!"

"…What's up? You're in a rush."

"I'd like a new set of equipment. Can you hook me up?"

"Well…technically, yes, but I'm gonna need a better idea of what you're looking for… Did something happen?"

"…I'm not sure myself. Could you come with me for a bit?"

"Seriously, what's this all about?"

Maple dragged Iz out so she could demonstrate her new skill in the open field.

For the next five days…

Iz spent all her in-game time in her workshop, thinking about Maple's gear, trying things out until she could make a prototype she was satisfied with.

"No…this gear isn't good enough for *that*…"

Similar mutterings could be heard at all hours.

Five days after Maple placed her order…

She logged in, and as she appeared in the Guild Home, Iz emerged from the workshop.

"I've finished your gear, Maple."

"You have?!"

"That's right. Take a look."

Iz opened her inventory, taking out a full suit of white armor, a great shield, a short sword, and a silver tiara.

Every piece of equipment was studded with blue gems.

The outfit screamed classic paladin, with the exception of the tiara.

"This really *will* make me look like a noble knight..."
Maple equipped it all, checking the stats.

Archangel Tiara X

[HP +250]

Archangel White Shield IX

[HP +300]

Archangel Holy Blade VIII

[HP +200]

Archangel Holy Armor IX

[HP +350]

"What are these roman numerals?" Maple asked.

"Those are enhancements that only appear on gear crafted with the Smithing skill. Unlike unique drops or gear you find in events, crafted gear doesn't come with skills, so this gives crafted equipment a way to keep up."

"Interesting..."

"The success rate for enhancements depends on the level of your Smithing skill, but you need some serious luck to get something all the way to the maximum X. We can talk payment and materials later. Making you stronger means opening more doors for us."

"Definitely! But if you need anything, just say the word!"

Maple was more than happy to pay her back.

Iz's gear was top-tier, no question.

Later, Iz let it slip that this set was two steps above what she'd made for Chrome, but Maple was too busy admiring her new toys to notice.

She was still at it when the other four guild members showed up.

"Mm? …Hot damn! That's the gear Iz has been working on? Nice! It looks great," Chrome said. Then he muttered, "Now I want some new gear…"

"I'm scared to ask why you wanted a new set, Maple…" Sally sighed.

"Good point." Kasumi nodded. "Was there something wrong with the gear you already had?"

Kanade just smiled. "You look great in white, too, Maple!" he declared.

"Hmm," Maple said. "I think the best way to explain is to demonstrate. In combat!"

Everyone agreed, eager to learn more.

Iz tagged along, wanting to see how the gear she'd made would hold up to what was coming.

"This place should be as good as any."

Maple had flown them all on Syrup, setting up in an area known for high spawn rates.

"All righty…let's go! Martyr's Devotion!"

Red damage effects appeared all over Maple.

And when they vanished, the area ten yards around Maple glowed faintly.

But that wasn't all.

Two white wings had appeared on Maple's back, and a dazzling ring floated above her head.

Moreover, her hair had taken on a beautiful gold color—and her eyes had become a deep shade of blue.

"""""What?!"""""

"That's what I said my first time seeing it."

"Ah-ha-ha... My whole look changes when I use the skill. Oh, here come the monsters."

Their brains had locked up for a second, but the party quickly recovered—as they reminded themselves that with Maple, anything was possible—and turned their attention to the battle at hand.

Their definition of normal was steadily changing the more time they spent around her.

"Don't worry about taking damage!"

"Allow me. It'll be a good demonstration for the others."

Iz stepped forward, letting a monster attack her.

But her HP bar didn't budge.

"Huh? How in the...?"

"It's Maple's skill. She can perpetually keep Cover up on every party member standing in the light's range...apparently."

"I have to pay a hefty chunk of HP when I activate the skill, though."

Like Hydra, Martyr's Devotion gave Maple several sub-skills.

The AOE Cover skill she was currently using was one of these. This skill meant that to defeat any member of Maple Tree, you first had to take out Maple.

And just as Hydra gave her Paralyze Shout, Martyr's Devotion had more powers she had yet to reveal.

But each of those required a significant HP sacrifice.

The catch was that with Maple's previous gear, she didn't have nearly enough HP to use these new skills. That's why she'd begged Iz for a new set.

Martyr's Devotion was a massive improvement on Benevolent Knight.

That extra quest was really no joke.

"So...this gives us all as much defense as Maple? Dear god."

As long as they were in range, they were safe—assuming Maple was up and at 'em.

Of course, taking Maple down was easier said than done.

The only viable strategy was spamming piercing attacks.

And those still had to actually *hit*.

Nobody could hit Sally, Chrome was great at parrying with his shield, and Kasumi was quite nimble in her own right.

Kanade was the only party member anyone could reasonably expect to hit.

"But, Maple, you've changed up your gear, right? Does that mean you don't have enough defense to blunt all incoming damage?"

"Don't worry! Even with no gear, I have over 1,000 VIT!"

""Ha-ha...seriously?""

Chrome and Kasumi just laughed out loud.

They were long past rational thought.

While riding Syrup back, Chrome said, "Maple, Sally, I talk about you guys from time to time on a game forum. Should I stop?"

"Hmm... I guess I don't mind," Sally said. "Everything I've told you is cool to make public."

"I'm with Sally! I mean..."

""Even if people know, it won't matter.""

Chrome could post everything he knew, and Sally would still be just as impossible to hit, and Maple would stay just as invulnerable.

Chrome didn't know how they'd earned their skills, so he couldn't disclose anything really important even if he wanted to.

It was no skin off their teeth either way.

----

126 Name: Anonymous Great Shielder
Sup

127 Name: Anonymous Spear Master
Yo...
You're in Maple's guild?!
Jealous! I hate you!

128 Name: Anonymous Greatsworder
Lucky.
I know we said to make contact with Sally, but you went too far!

129 Name: Anonymous Archer
Give us deets.
You've gotta have something!
Not asking you to spill guild secrets or anything.

130 Name: Anonymous Spear Master
Being in the inner circle prob makes it tough to share.
But share what you can!

131 Name: Anonymous Mage
Please

132 Name: Anonymous Great Shielder
Will do.
First, about Sally...

Like the rumors, hella dodgy.
From what I can tell, it ain't a skill.
Might be something else going on, but...
All I can say is, I've seen her fight a lot of monsters, and I haven't seen her take any damage yet.
And she gets some sorta aura going...

133 Name: Anonymous Archer
So it *was* Sally who ran wild during that event?
The blue demon who dodged everything?

134 Name: Anonymous Greatsworder
And now she's evolving.
What aura?

135 Name: Anonymous Archer
Hmm.
Sally likely has her share of mystery skills.
Maybe not as many as Maple, but...

136 Name: Anonymous Great Shielder
Speaking of Maple...
She went off on her own the last few days.

And when she came back...

137 Name: Anonymous Greatsworder

Don't leave us hanging!

138 Name: Anonymous Spear Master
Spill it!

139 Name: Anonymous Mage
What happened?!

140 Name: Anonymous Great Shielder

She's an angel.

141 Name: Anonymous Archer
Yeah, we know *that*.

142 Name: Anonymous Mage
Not news

143 Name: Anonymous Greatsworder
Always has been

144 Name: Anonymous Spear Master
Obviously.

145 Name: Anonymous Great Shielder
Okay, fair.

Lemme rephrase.

Maple came back with a skill that gives her wings, a halo, blond hair, and blue eyes.

146 Name: Anonymous Spear Master
WUT

147 Name: Anonymous Mage
That's whatcha get for taking your eyes off her.

148 Name: Anonymous Greatsworder
How? Where do you even find this skill?

149 Name: Anonymous Great Shielder
Dunno.

Skill name is Martyr's Devotion.
It lets her indefinitely Cover every party member in range.

So if Maple uses it...

Her entire party becomes functionally immortal.

150 Name: Anonymous Greatsworder
She's obtained her second form.
Have they officially made her the last boss yet?

151 Name: Anonymous Spear Master
Hell seems lukewarm by comparison.

Don't take your eyes off her again.
She'll come back with a third form.
Guaranteed.

152 Name: Anonymous Great Shielder

And apparently even with no gear on, her VIT is over 1,000.

153 Name: Anonymous Archer
I don't even know what's what anymore.

154 Name: Anonymous Spear Master
That's just freakish.
Is her body made of steel?
Orichalcum?

155 Name: Anonymous Spear Master
She hasn't even been playing that long.
When the rumors first started up, she hadn't made it to the second stratum yet.

There's gotta be something on the first stratum.

156 Name: Anonymous Great Shielder
I thought the same thing...
But if that's true, shouldn't we have a second or third Maple by now?

157 Name: Anonymous Mage
Fair.

There must be some reason only Maple can do it, but I have no idea what that might be.

They all gave it some thought, but nobody could figure out how Maple had gotten her skills.

CHAPTER 3

Defense Build and Helping Out

The day after Maple revealed to the guild her angel form and absolutely broken new power…

Chrome and Iz were in the Guild Home, deep in conversation.

"Maple sure is getting stronger fast."

"Yeah. Never a boring moment."

"It's just…you know…"

"Mm?"

"I'm like a crappy knockoff version of her!"

"…………Hard to argue with."

It was a simple fact that both his offense and defense were way lower than Maple's.

His only real advantage was raw gaming ability.

"I've gotta find something to prove I'm worth keeping around…"

"Can't blame you for feeling that way."

As they spoke, the door opened, and Maple came in.

"Speak of the devil…"

"You were talking about me?"

"In a manner of speaking."

"I was hoping to get some good skills like you did."

Chrome didn't want *her* skills—he wanted some of his own. Maple beamed at the idea.

He asked her what the secret to getting good skills was, but she answered honestly—she'd found most of them by simply exploring. Not particularly helpful advice.

"Hmm… I'm a little busy today… Oh, I know! I can lend you Syrup. Anything helps, right?"

Maple pulled up her menu, removed her ring, then took it out of her inventory and gave it to Chrome.

"Uh…you're sure? This is important, right? What if I don't give it back?"

"Would you actually do something like that?"

"Never." He was very firm.

He had no intention of doing anything of the sort.

"Then it'll be fine!" Maple said, grinning.

Chrome spent a while lecturing her on the importance of not lending out valuables, even to guild members.

But Maple clearly wanted to help Chrome, and eventually he gave in and accepted the ring.

Out in the field, he was still mulling over what had happened at the Guild Home.

"I'd better warn Sally, too…"

Chrome was happy Maple trusted him, but he worried she was a little too trusting.

"…Gotta make sure nobody takes advantage of that."

Maple was having a good time playing, but…she lacked experience.

There were still a lot of ways to have "fun" she didn't know about.

She probably only had a faint idea how malicious some players could be.

And keeping players like that at bay was one of the few things Chrome could do that Maple couldn't.

"Plus, I wanna make sure she can enjoy herself without worrying."

Chrome continued west as he crossed the field.

"Well, since I've borrowed it, I might as well use it. I owe her that much, at least."

Chrome summoned Syrup but let it walk alongside him without making it giant.

The skill that made it fly was Maple's, not his, so Giganticize served little use.

"Oh, more monsters."

Chrome drew his short sword and braced his great shield.

They were facing three boars.

And he had only one shield.

If multiple boars attacked at once, that would hurt.

"Gah! These blows would just bounce off Maple!"

He slashed at a charging boar, then quickly backed away.

Red sparks flew.

The boar gave chase, but he knocked it back with his shield.

"Thrust!"

Chrome activated a skill, and his blade shot forward.

The strike hit the staggering boar, robbing it of HP.

And all the while, Chrome's HP was slowly refilling.

Great shielders were notoriously short on offensive options, but it was no fluke that Chrome had come in ninth in the first event.

He had one skill your average player didn't.

Battle Healing

Recover 1% HP every ten seconds during combat.

This skill, combined with his high defense, had been how he'd managed to claw his way to ninth.

Compared with Maple, Chrome might have looked weak, but by the standards of the average player, he was pretty damn tough.

The first event's top ten all had some sort of powerful skill.

Maple's were just especially ridiculous, so she'd drawn all the attention.

Making sure to let Syrup fight so it could share the XP, Chrome headed farther west.

He eventually reached the western wastelands.

"I haven't explored out this way yet, so that's today's goal."

After poking around for a while, he stumbled upon an old grave.

Any player worth their salt knew things like this were worth investigating.

Chrome was no exception.

But his eyes were locked on the grave itself, and he failed to notice the pit right in front of it—and before he knew it, he was falling.

Down below, Chrome picked himself up.

There was a shaft leading deeper in.

"Hmm? Is this a hidden dungeon or...?"

He scanned his surroundings and saw that Syrup had followed him down.

"Wow… Does Maple's luck rub off?"

Chrome felt like all weirdness stemmed from Maple.

But there weren't any mystery Maple shenanigans at work here; this was all his own doing.

Sally, Maple, Kasumi, Kanade, and Iz all had something unique to them.

So did Chrome.

Specifically, he had died a lot.

Having picked the game's "worst" option, he'd struggled with it at first. Before he'd mastered the great shield, his low damage output had frequently left him surrounded and unable to stave off death.

Learning the tricks of great shielding had taken him ages.

And all that time, he'd been racking up his death count.

The crucible in which he'd been forged.

Making up for lack of talent with time and hard work.

Battle Healing had been a random acquisition he had made at one point on his long journey of death.

Death came hand in hand with skills and techniques.

And this dungeon was called the Grave of the Dead.

Neither Maple nor Sally could have entered.

Only players like Chrome could enter—players who had died and revived more than one thousand times.

Chrome continued down the passage.

Syrup plodded along behind.

"Let's see what's waiting for us. Might kill me, but oh well."

Each death came with a penalty; you'd lose a portion of the XP you'd built up and some of your skill proficiency. But Chrome had been overcoming that penalty all this time and hadn't fretted over it in a long while.

He inspected the walls around him. They were crumbling, seemingly ready to collapse at any moment.

They didn't look man-made.

"If this is below a grave, am I gonna be fighting something undead?"

A reasonable prediction.

And one that proved entirely accurate. Not long after he spoke, the shaft opened up into a larger room, and a bunch of skeletons lumbered out.

They were equipped with rusty spears and swords, which was not terribly intimidating.

Low-level monsters, trying to win with numbers.

Chrome had Syrup join the fight, dividing their attention, and successfully dispatched the horde.

"Oh-ho. Syrup leveled up."

Chrome gave it a potion to restore the HP it had lost, then checked the pet's new skill.

"It learned Cover? Hmm. Your skill tree has a lot of overlap with great shields, huh?"

Maple didn't often let Syrup join battles, so it was still fairly low-level.

Adventuring with Chrome gave it more chances to grow.

By the time he gave it back to Maple, it would likely have even more levels and skills.

"I guess leveling her pet's a decent way to thank her for the loaner."

Chrome decided to let Syrup take the lead in battles for more experience.

They headed deeper in. Syrup defeated the bulk of the enemies, quickly growing in strength.

"Mm? More new skills?"

A few fights later, Chrome checked Syrup's stats and found two new additions.

Mother Nature

Raise the earth or grow vines and trees to attack or defend.

Spirit Cannon

Can only be used when Giganticized.
Frontal ranged attack.

"Okay, you're pretty much stronger than I am now. Man...I want a partner of my own."

A few fights later, Chrome reached the deepest part of the dungeon.

Before him stood a giant door—clearly the entrance to the boss room.

"This place was on the long side, but there weren't exactly any tough enemies hanging around... Maybe I can pull this off."

After concluding that the dungeon wasn't particularly difficult, he decided to give it a go.

The boss room was huge—big enough to make Syrup giant and still have space to spare.

A short while after they crossed the threshold, a skeleton rose at the other end of the room.

Unlike the previous skeletons, this one was equipped with extremely fancy (albeit still ancient) armor and a longsword. Two pale-blue lights glowed in the sockets of its skull, like wisps.

"Whew… First time trying to solo a boss, but…I guess I'm not actually solo."

Chrome had Syrup use Giganticize, and then he got the battle rolling.

"Mother Nature!"

Thick vines spawned from the ground around Syrup, quickly grasping at the boss, but they were all stopped by a glowing pale-blue barrier that covered the boss's body.

"Guess we've gotta get past that first."

Leaving Syrup in the rear, Chrome stepped toward the boss——who stepped toward him.

"Shield Attack!"

The barrier stopped Chrome's blow as expected, but he just wanted to check if cumulative damage could break the thing.

"Here we go…!"

Deflecting a longsword swing with his shield, Chrome hacked at the barrier with his own blade.

But barrier breaking was hardly the purview of a tank, so he wasn't really making much headway.

And if Chrome's own equipment took too much damage, it would break.

Given how hard the boss was hitting, drawing out this fight would be unwise.

Figuring he needed a new approach, Chrome dodged an attack and shouted, "Syrup! Spirit Cannon!"

Syrup fired a bright-white laser beam.

He'd used it once before this final battle, so Chrome knew the timing and range and was able to leap out of the way.

"Try that on for size!"

As the light faded, he heard a shattering sound.

The barrier was down.

But that wasn't entirely a good thing.

There was a rattling noise, and the boss stabbed its sword into the ground.

Skeletons started pouring out of all four corners of the room.

Alone, Chrome would easily have been overwhelmed—but he had Syrup with him.

Syrup managed to occupy most of the skeletons, making it easier for Chrome to focus on the boss.

Keeping one eye on Syrup's health, he chipped away at the boss's health.

Syrup managed to land the odd blow, too.

As long as he could avoid the boss's attacks, Battle Healing would take care of any damage the skeleton hordes managed to do.

He could take care of them once the boss slowed down a bit.

Steady play kept the advantage on Chrome's side.

"Shield Attack!"

The boss had no shield, so it was easy to land blows—and that was a huge help.

Reeling from the knockback, the boss was totally exposed.

"You don't have *that* much HP, do you?"

Focusing too much on his combination attacks could leave him open to a nasty counter, so Chrome backed off after a few hits—but even that much had brought the boss down to nearly half health.

But only because Syrup was with him.

Syrup's Mother Nature attacks were doing a fair bit of damage. And the incredibly helpful pet was keeping the bulk of the skeletons busy; without Syrup, this likely would never have been much of a fight at all.

"I better thank her for this later... Flame Slash!"

After his blade became wreathed in flame, he landed a diagonal strike on the boss's torso.

And with that, the boss's health finally dipped below 50 percent.

The boss retreated to its starting point, calling the skeletons to its side.

And they collapsed to the ground—black orbs emerged from each for the boss to absorb.

No more skeletons lumbered out from the corners of the room.

A pitch-black aura emanated from the boss, taking the shape of an even bigger skeleton.

One hand of this bony giant gripped a very long sword—one third the length of the room. The other held a battle-ax.

"Second form, huh? Maple's is way scarier. Maybe you should try copying her?"

Chrome readied his shield as he made the comment.

And so the battle entered its second phase.

"Let's get this done...!"

Chrome stepped forward, shield raised.

The boss swung its sword in response, but Chrome didn't try to block it—he dodged instead.

A moment later, his great shield caught the ax as it came in from the other direction. The impact knocked him backward.

"Gah...!"

Chrome checked his shield.

Unlike Maple's and Sally's gear, Chrome's would break if he pushed it past its limits.

He was still good for now, but if he kept taking blows that powerful, the risk was very real.

He pulled back out of the boss's attack range.

"Spirit Cannon!"

The boss couldn't reach Syrup, so Chrome had it use the laser-beam skill.

However, the boss crossed the sword and ax, successfully blocking all damage.

"Gotta get in close, huh?"

They weren't beating this thing with ranged attacks alone. Chrome pressed forward once more.

"Mother Nature!"

The boss crossed its weapons again to block the incoming vines. But while it was busy with Syrup's attacks, Chrome dashed underneath, rapidly closing the distance.

"Flame Slash!"

As his blow landed, the boss's sword turned toward him—but Chrome had a great shield.

The attack couldn't hurt him.

The moment Mother Nature ran out, the boss would have both weapons free—so Chrome couldn't afford to waste a second.

"Thrust!"

His short sword pierced the boss's armor, reducing it to 20 percent health.

The moment it crossed that threshold, jet-black spikes shot out of the boss.

Chrome raised his shield on pure reflex, defending himself, but the sword struck it a moment later—and it shattered.

"Iz is gonna be furious!"

The spikes were a onetime thing and soon vanished. Chrome dived in, slashing with his short sword, trying to do what damage he could.

Then Syrup's Mother Nature ran out.

Without his shield, Chrome was fully exposed to both sword and ax.

He kept moving, letting only the sword hit him, attacking the boss as much as he could.

Both were carving chunks out of each other's health with their blades.

The boss had raised its ax high, and while Chrome's attention was on the sword, it scored a clean hit on his back. A huge hit to his HP bar—and it blew off his armor to boot.

But he was still standing.

Indomitable Guardian had left him with a single point of health. One of many vital survival skills Chrome had in his toolbox that could make all the difference in a close fight.

"Flame Slash!"

Already at his limit, Chrome swung his blade.

However, the boss still had 10 percent health left.

Its weapons were hurtling toward him.

Battle Healing wouldn't restore his health in time.

"Spirit Light!"

This was the skill Chrome had used his medals to procure.

The ultimate ace up his sleeve.

He was wreathed in a holy light that nullified all damage for ten full seconds.

"I ain't dying yet!"

Ignoring all incoming attacks, he mustered everything he

could and channeled it into his offense. The boss did the same—but couldn't do him any harm.

Chrome's short sword slashed diagonally across the boss's face. In an instant, the blue light in its eyes vanished.

Within a few moments, the pitch-black skeleton turned to light...and was gone.

"Whew...that was close. Great shielders really oughtta stick to defending."

As he sat down heavily, a magic circle appeared—along with a coffin.

Chrome scrambled backward, calling over Syrup.

"If that's a monster, cover me... I'd better chug a potion."

Once his HP was back, he carefully lifted the coffin lid.

Inside was a skeleton, wearing a set of bloodred armor.

It wasn't moving.

"Huh? I-is this a reward?"

Chrome gingerly reached in and took the gear for his inventory.

"Unique...series? Whoa..."

Bloodstained Skull

[VIT +25] [Indestructible]
Skill: Soul Eater

Bloodstained Bone Armor

[VIT +25] [HP +100] [Indestructible]
Skill: Dead or Alive

Headhunter

[STR +30] [Indestructible]
Skill: Life Eater

Wrath Wraith Wall

[VIT +20] [HP +100] [Indestructible]
Skill: Soul Syphon

"So OP! The names and the look of the set make it seem totally cursed, though. Also, *is* this a short sword? Looks more like a cleaver."

Chrome went ahead and put on the new gear.

The lower half of his face was covered in a bloody skull.

The armor might have been bone white...once.

Like the name implied, the bloody cleaver looked like it had severed many a head.

Even the shield had a skeleton motif.

"Let's check out these skills and then...head on home."

Soul Eater

Recover 10% of max HP after felling a monster or player.

Dead or Alive

When HP becomes 0, 50% odds of surviving at 1 HP.

Life Eater

Whenever dealing damage, recover HP equal to one third of damage dealt.

Soul Syphon

Recover 3% HP when taking damage from an attack.

Chrome read through the skills, put Syrup back in the ring, stepped onto the magic circle, and left the dungeon behind.

A few days after Chrome took the first step on his journey to stop being a regular person…

…there was a brief maintenance outage, and the skill Shearing was added.

Like the name implied, it was a skill…for shearing things. Nothing else!

To accompany the skill, sheep had been added to certain areas.

According to Iz, these provided good materials, and they should collect them if they got a chance.

Maple and Kasumi had nothing better to do, so they set out across the first-stratum prairie.

"I came along because I had some free time, but will we be okay with just Shearing?"

"Not 'we,' Kasumi. Only you have the skill!"

Maple had put everything into defense, so she was unable to acquire Shearing.

Her job on this outing was to use Paralyze Shout and stop the sheep in their tracks.

Sheep HP was pretty low, so they needed a way to snare them without doing damage.

And Maple was perfect for that role.

"Not seeing any sheep with wool left…"

"Yes. Seems like other players have already shorn them."

They spotted a bunch of post-cut sheep, but no normal ones.

Their search went on for a good half hour.

"There's some!"

Kasumi pointed at a group of three sheep up ahead.

"Paralyze Shout!"

Maple immediately tried to paralyze them, but she wasn't quite in range and caught only one.

When they approached, the other two sheep ran away.

"Well, let's take care of this one. Shear!"

Kasumi used the skill, and the sheep's wool vanished—and was conveniently added to her inventory.

"That's clearly not enough…"

"Yeah…probably not."

If they showed up with one unit of wool, Iz wouldn't be able to make anything.

"Hmm… On my own, I can probably catch a running sheep.

I'm not…entirely lacking in skills that could stop them. I'm gonna give it a try solo."

"Okay! Have fun!"

Kasumi ran off after the sheep.

Leaving Maple and a shorn, paralyzed sheep behind.

"……………"

Maple glanced at the sheep.

It looked soft.

Kasumi was chasing after a sheep.

"Superspeed!"

It was fast enough that she had to use one of her ace in the holes to catch it.

And it seemed likely that Shearing wouldn't work if she couldn't find a way to stop it.

"Worth a shot, though… Shear!"

Figuring it was futile, she used Shearing while running parallel to the sheep…

And it was neatly shorn.

She skidded to a stop.

"Even on the go, it'll work as long as you're in range, huh? How very gamelike."

She checked her inventory, and she definitely had more wool.

The rest of the sheep had fled in a different direction. She looked but couldn't find them again.

She headed back to Maple, secure in the knowledge that nothing could harm her friend.

But when she got there, she found a mysterious white sphere instead.

"Huh?"

Kasumi drew her katana, approaching with caution.

"Is this...wool?"

Kasumi reached out and touched it, confirming it was definitely wool.

"Shear!"

Which meant the skill was worth trying.

And it worked like a charm! The giant wool sphere became ten pieces of wool in her inventory.

And there was a clang as Maple fell to the ground.

"Maple... You were...inside that thing?"

"Not...exactly. That...*was* me."

"Wh-what do you mean?"

"............I just...tried a thing."

Maple did not explain further.

"I...am so lost. But I get the sense it's better if I just don't ask."

Kasumi could take a hint, so she said no more.

"I can now make wool every twenty-four hours, so make sure to Shear me then!"

"Uh, okay. Sure."

They climbed aboard Syrup and headed back to the Guild Home.

Along the way, Maple checked her new skill again.

Sheep Eater

Back at the Guild Home, Kasumi and Chrome sat down together, talking.

Specifically about Maple and wool.

"I took my eyes off her for one minute, and she got yet another new skill."

"A friend of mine warned me never to take my eyes off her again," Chrome said. "I think I'm getting used to it, though."

"You are?"

"I may have started following in her footsteps…"

He waved a hand at his new gear.

It certainly was a step away from the norm.

"Then what would it take to surprise you?" Kasumi asked.

Chrome thought about this. It took a while.

"Uh…I guess if she sailed away into the air without warning, turned into a cloud, and started dropping lightning bolts?" he said, making it *sound* like a joke.

"Ha-ha-ha! Surely, *that* won't happen."

"Yeah, agreed. Oh, say, did you see the message from the admins?"

Kasumi shook her head.

Chrome quickly filled her in.

"Third event's in two weeks."

"They're pumping these out now, huh? What's the format?"

"Event-limited monsters show up, and we're collecting their drops. Individual and guild rewards are based on the number we collect."

And the minimum threshold for the guild reward varied depending on the guild size.

Maple's guild had been created with the lowest-ranking Glowbug Seal, so their threshold was on the low end.

But there was also an individual player ranking, with rewards based on personal performance.

And there was no gifting drops.

These drops wouldn't even appear in player inventories at all; the count was simply registered to your account.

"…Might be tough, then."

"…I thought the same thing."

They both meant *for Maple*.

She'd done very well in the previous events, but that was down to sheer strength, and it had not taken much time.

This format made it impossible for her to do well.

"I'm on the slow side myself, but...there's always someone worse."

Maple Tree began preparing for the third event.

◆□◆□◆□◆□◆

On one such day, Iz and Kanade were chatting in the Guild Home.

"We're basically support for the other four."

Iz was noncombat support.

Meanwhile, Kanade was the sole player who occupied the rear of the party's battle formation.

"I've learned some attack magic, too, but...doesn't seem like there's much call for it. Perhaps I should try a different tactic."

The four front-liners could take out any monster before Kanade got a chance to attack, so he was focused on skills to buff ally stats and recovery magic.

"I'm the only one with a staff, which means I can learn things the rest of you can't."

Sally had learned *some* magic, but Kanade had a lot more spells available to him.

And in this guild, that was his exclusive domain.

"If I can buff them, they'll be able to take anything on."

"Yeah, they're good like that. Oh, that reminds me... How's that gear working out? I made a couple of adjustments... You liking it?"

This was the original reason Iz had asked him here. Kanade was already nodding enthusiastically.

He'd bought a couple of things to improve his starting gear, but by the second event, he still looked like a newbie. Iz had hooked him up with some proper threads.

A newsboy cap as red as his hair.

The rest was mostly red and black and looked less like equipment than ordinary clothes.

Maple's wool had been used to help improve it.

Every piece raised INT and MP, so just wearing this gear buffed Kanade considerably.

"I'm not exactly the armor type."

With his new-and-improved gear on, Kanade left the Guild Home.

His goal for the day was to learn Magic Barrier.

At the moment, Kanade was the guild member racking up the most new skills.

Opponents would have to take him out to stop the support and recovery magic.

But that might mean taking out angel-Maple first.

In that form, Maple's VIT would be buffing Kanade, too.

And the instant her HP dropped, Kanade would be ready with heals.

Soon the most sensible plan would be to just *not* fight Maple Tree at all.

Perhaps that day was already here.

Meanwhile, at the edge of the second stratum…

Sally was in a forest.

"Whew… Haven't taken any damage so far, but…might be high time I prepare myself for the possibility."

She'd picked up a number of new skills over the past few days.

But this was nowhere near her ideal build.

"Plus, I've gotta level up Oboro."

In this forest, you didn't have to walk far to find more monsters.

Sally was focusing on evasion, damaging monsters a bit, and then letting Oboro finish them.

After grinding like that awhile, Oboro leveled up.

"Whew… Let's see… Oh?"

Oboro's new skill put a grin on her face, and she rubbed its head.

"Maybe I don't need to worry about taking damage after all!"

With that, she stopped training Oboro and headed back to town.

Chrome was in the second-stratum desert.

"This is nuts! Ain't nothin' gonna kill me!"

He was taking attacks with his shield, then hacking away with the cleaver.

That alone was making his HP skyrocket—and the effects of Battle Healing stacked on top of that.

And if he ever found himself in real danger, he could just bust out Spirit Light.

Chrome dispatched the final monster and sheathed his weapon.

"Maple's gear is definitely a unique series, too. That shield and sword definitely have skills on 'em. But doesn't seem like the armor has anything…"

The Indestructible thing was also huge.

No more need to maintain his gear.

"I bet Maple's got Indestructible on hers, too."

She actually had something way more terrifying, but Chrome was blissfully unaware of that.

"Let's hunt a bit longer."

Chrome might have been a great shielder, but solo hunts were now also completely safe for him.

Neither of Maple Tree's great shielders was anything close to "normal" anymore.

This class was not known for being any use on the offensive.

Elsewhere, Kasumi was also engaged in combat.

She was the Maple Tree member with the most consistent DPS.

Sally used daggers, while Chrome and Maple had their short swords. That meant Kasumi's sword gave her the longest reach on their front line.

She had the highest STR in the guild, and her AGI was up there, too.

Her build meant her defense was a bit of a concern, but angel-Maple had solved that problem.

It was all very...stable.

"Right... Better head on back."

Then she realized she had an unread message.

"From Maple... Let's see..."

She opened it up and read the contents.

Due west of the second-stratum town.
Come Shear me.
I would appreciate it if you could hurry.

"Um, huh? Well, no reason not to..."

Kasumi ran off in search of Maple.

Ten minutes earlier...

Maple had gone west to experiment with her wool-growing skill.

When she found a good spot, she yelled, "Wool Up!" and her vision filled with an expanse of white fluff.

"Definitely doesn't seem like I can control the volume of it... Hmm. Mm! Hmph!"

Maple burrowed diagonally downward and managed to pop her head out of the wool ball.

And her arms and legs.

"Can I move like this?"

That might not make a difference.

But since she could now see monsters attacking her in this form, she realized something else.

"Does this wool have my full defense value?"

It did.

As long as it was attacked, the wool was considered a part of her and shared her stats.

"So if I'm holed up in the wool, I'm pretty OP until someone Shears me?"

Maple tried to think of how that might be useful but didn't really get anywhere. Then she tried to be less woolly and realized something important.

"Augh! I can't do anything about this on my own?!"

She could see some players passing in the distance, frowning at the mystery ball of wool.

It wouldn't be long before she was exposed—and on all fours.

She quickly sent a note to Kasumi.

"T-time to hide!"

She burrowed back into the wool and sprayed poison in all directions so no other players could get near.

"Augh! Now Kasumi can't, either!"

The realization came too late.

She could hear a lot of voices outside, but nobody could Shear her through the poison.

After a while, the poison vanished, and Kasumi collected her, but by then everyone knew it was Maple, and her crazy stunts were a hot topic on the forums once again.

----

280 Name: Anonymous Greatsworder
Maple back at it again, huh?

281 Name: Anonymous Spear Master
So I hear.
Eyewitness reports claim she turned into a giant fur ball.

282 Name: Anonymous Mage
There's no way you can do that while playing normally.

283 Name: Anonymous Spear Master
I suppose not, no.

284 Name: Anonymous Archer
Did the sheep get to her? Did she become one?

285 Name: Anonymous Spear Master
I feel like it's an oddly fitting fate.

286 Name: Anonymous Greatsworder
Fur balls seem harmless.
They're just fluffy.

287 Name: Anonymous Mage
But there was poison gushing out of it.

288 Name: Anonymous Spear Master
Is it some sort of sea urchin?

289 Name: Anonymous Archer

Maple spurts poison when she's in trouble.

290 Name: Anonymous Greatsworder
I think she'd be plenty strong even without poison.

291 Name: Anonymous Spear Master
Well, there is her natural enemy, piercing damage.

292 Name: Anonymous Mage
Mm? Wait, how does the damage work in fur-ball form?
Would you be able to hit her while she's inside?

293 Name: Anonymous Archer
She's slain her natural enemy.

294 Name: Anonymous Spear Master
She's the top of the food chain.
Look out for the fur-ball fortress.

They resolved to ask Chrome if he showed up, and thus…time passed.

CHAPTER 4

Defense Build and the Third Event

Maple logged in, appearing at the Guild Home. There, she found Sally, Kanade, and Iz at the entrance.

"The event's begun!" Maple declared excitedly.

"It's only been five hours, and the top players are already at five digits! Chrome and Kasumi are out hunting."

There was no time compression for this event, so Maple wasn't planning on spending too many hours on it. She was just going to do what she could.

"Wow…everyone's so good…!"

The four of them were still at 0. Iz in particular was only planning on dipping her toe in the water this time.

"I've got next to no attack skills, but my STR ain't too shabby."

You could defeat some enemies by hitting them with a smithing hammer.

And obviously, she had way more STR than Maple.

"Well, we'd better head out!"

"Yeah."

Leaving Iz behind, they turned to go—but Iz stopped them.

She handed Sally and Maple some new gear.

"I made these from the wool. Supposedly, the event drop rates go up based on the amount of wool used."

And thanks to Maple, they had more than enough wool.

Kanade's regular gear was already made from wool, so he was set.

The gear Iz handed Sally was fluffy, but not so loose that it might impede her movements. It was mostly white—as one might expect, given the materials.

Maple's gear was even more sheeplike.

Pure-white, full-body gear, every bit as fluffy as an unshorn sheep.

"Obviously, I can't make armor out of wool, so..."

Given the need for attack skills, Maple kept her usual black shield and sword. These didn't match the adorable outfit, but there wasn't a lot she could do to help that.

Iz didn't mention this, but the look of these outfits was based on nothing but her desire to see Maple wear some soft, fluffy clothing.

Armor might not have been doable, but she could certainly have made more...ordinary clothing.

It purely came down to her personal aesthetics.

The three of them left the guild together but split up soon after.

Sticking together would just mean farming fewer drops overall, while splitting up allowed them to improve both the guild total and their individual scores.

Maple was riding Syrup and examining a screen filled with info on how many points were needed to get rewards.

It also had a picture of the monsters they were targeting—red bulls.

"I'm so slow, though. This really isn't my kinda event..."

Even riding Syrup, she didn't hold a candle to Sally.

She found a reward she wanted, set a point requirement as her target, and decided to enjoy the event on those terms.

"Just gotta get enough to earn this skill!"

She read the skill description one more time, then closed the screen. She glanced at the ground below and saw some red bulls.

"Hydra!"

She dropped a poison dragon off Syrup's side, then jumped down after it to collect her spoils. She'd attacked from outside the monster's detection range, so there was no chance of it fleeing.

And her attacks were strong enough that as long as she hit, they were as good as dead.

But the conditions to wield that power were pretty strict.

"Hmm… What if I run into enemies that have Poison Nullification?"

Opponents like that would really limit her options.

Frankly, she might actually be better off running away if she encountered enemies like that. Overreliance on poison could definitely become a major problem for her in the future.

And she'd used her poison and paralysis attacks so often that nearly every player in the game was familiar with her capabilities.

There was no telling when the admins would hold another PVP event, but there were likely a lot of players leveling Poison Resist in preparation.

Any strong player would be aware of the need for anti-Maple measures.

Plus, there were definitely players out there who could take out Maple one-on-one, if they planned for it and came prepared.

"Come to think of it, now that I'm level thirty, I can actually add a second skill to my equipment."

But with her extreme build, the range of skills she could acquire was pretty limited.

She'd yet to put a skill on her armor at all—and now there were two slots available.

"No use thinking about it now!"

Maple flew around the field, occasionally making it rain poison.

"Not that many bulls, huh? I wonder if there's a bigger herd somewhere else."

The admin posting said they could spawn anywhere except underwater or in boss rooms, so Maple decided she'd be better off heading where other players wouldn't be.

Half an hour later...

Maple had kept an eye on the ground the whole time, but opportunities to rack up points had been few and far between.

Her speed was really working against her.

But she kept up her spirits, finding any bulls she could.

It helped that Maple found flying around on Syrup inherently enjoyable.

"After I'm done bull hunting, maybe I should take a walk with you, Syrup! I've been doing so many quests, I haven't really had time to just look around."

Maple thought about this a little more and decided to put the bull search on hold for the day and enjoy a midair stroll with Syrup.

The ground might be filled with bull slaughter, but up above, Maple was thoroughly enjoying the game on her own terms.

Meanwhile, the admins were watching the event closely, vigilant for the appearance of any bugs.

"Keep an eye on Maple," one warned. "She regularly does things beyond the capacity of human reason."

"Yeah, I'm on it."

They were constantly considering nerfing her.

Her defense and Devour were both broken to begin with, and now Syrup was a whole new source of concern.

"She's single-handedly disrupting the game's balance... There are so many things we'd have to fix. This mystery flight thing is just the tip of the iceberg."

"For sure."

"But...part of me thinks, why bother?"

"Explain."

"I mean, Maple's a star player now. Everyone's eyes are on her..."

And a lot of new players had joined, hoping to be like her one day.

Every time Maple did something ridiculous, micro-transaction sales skyrocketed as players tried to buy their way into competing with her. XP or skill proficiency boosts sold particularly well.

As a result, the admins were leaning toward simply leaving her be.

With this many people watching her every move, an obvious nerf might provoke an outcry.

"We've made adjustments to the third stratum so Maple flying won't wreck the event."

"Meaning just leave her alone otherwise?"

"Yeah, we'll simply observe. Besides, when we're not desperately trying to nerf her, she's basically just another cute player, right?"

"We've adjusted acquisition on Absolute Defense. There's no risk of new Maples becoming a commonplace sight. We're good as long as nothing unprecedented happens. And there are several other players as good as she is."

"She's bad news for my heart, but...so far, it isn't a *real* problem. For now."

"Yes, for now..."

That was a loaded phrase, but either way...

Unbeknownst to Maple, she'd earned the admins' tacit approval.

◆□◆□◆□◆□◆

Maple spent a while just savoring her flying "walk" with Syrup, but then she heard a *ding*—an incoming message.

"Hmm? Wonder who it's from."

She checked the sender's name and found she actually had *three* messages.

From Chrome, Kasumi, and Iz.

As if they'd compared notes, all three messages said basically the same thing.

They were all encouraging her to do her best in this event.

"I'm taking them out as soon as I find them, but…I'm just not fast enough."

She sent a reply saying she'd do what she could, then flew on.

"Maybe I'll find some outside this prairie? Let's try those mountains!"

She headed toward the distant peaks.

All three had messaged Maple because each had independently had the same realization.

They were letting her play on her own.

So they suggested she focus on the event to prevent her getting mixed up in anything weird.

There was no telling what might happen if they took their eyes off her.

Weird wasn't necessarily good.

All three had chosen a roundabout way to keep her under control.

Sometime later, Maple reached the mountains.

"There's nobody else here, huh?"

The steep slopes were dotted with trees—and not many bulls.

Like the admins said, they *did* spawn here...but there wasn't much space for them to do so in numbers.

Even with no competition, this would not be an efficient hunting ground.

But for Maple, any other player could easily beat her to a target, so she'd never been remotely efficient—meaning this was actually a modest improvement.

"If I've got this place to myself, maybe that's for the best!"

She put Syrup back in her ring and started climbing the mountain, killing bulls on her way.

Since she had a full set of woolly garments, she was at least keeping pace with players who didn't.

"I wonder if Kasumi and Sally have reached the top ranks by now..."

Those two had the most mobility in Maple Tree.

And with wool gear, they could easily harvest two to three times what Maple had.

"I'll just take it at my speed. At this pace, I should be able to get that skill!"

As she spoke, the rocks at her feet crumbled.

"Augh?!"

She lost her balance and grabbed on to a nearby tree for support.

"Augh...it's no use..."

This support lasted only a few seconds.

Maple tried to think of a way to extricate herself from this predicament...but before she did, she started rolling down the slope.

Tumbling head over heels, picking up speed, bouncing off boulders in her path, crashing through thickets, the world in view spinning madly.

"Augh! S-somebody stop me!"

Maple rolled downhill for quite a while, but eventually she slammed into something with a loud clang.

"Urp... So dizzy... Good thing I put all my points in VIT. I'd better be more careful."

If she hadn't made a defense build, she'd have been forcibly sent back to town.

But during the tumble, she'd used up all her Devours.

"Ugh...fine. I'll just hunt a little bit more and call it a day... Hmm?"

She got up and looked around, then realized she'd been stopped by a tall tree.

"Wow, that's...huge. Oh!"

Looking closer, she noticed something. The base of the tree was split...in the shape of a great shield.

Clearly, the victim of her final Devour.

"I-I'm sorry!"

She peered into the crack and spotted a distinctive hollow— one she hadn't made. And in that hollow was a piece of rusty gear.

Upon further investigation, Maple saw a faint glow.

The hollow ran all the way up the inside of the tree—suggesting this gear had fallen down the shaft.

She grabbed it for a closer look.

"Let's see, the item's name is...Bygone Dream?"

No skill. Not able to be equipped.

No effects, no item description.

Maple couldn't see any use for it beyond decorating the Guild Home.

"I guess I might as well keep it? Can I heal the tree?"

Maple switched to her white gear and drank a potion to restore her HP.

"Okay! Devotion's Light!"

There was a violent red spray as Maple took damage.

A few moments later, light poured out of her palm, enveloping the tree.

"...No effect? That's the strongest heal I've got, too..."

She had several healing abilities included in the Martyr's Devotion skill set.

But none of them could restore her own health.

"I'm...really sorry!"

She bowed to the tree again, then turned to go.

"Better get out of this forest and then take Syrup home."

She switched back to her regular gear and exited the forest, cutting down several more bulls on the way.

Meanwhile, Chrome finished off a bull, then paused in his tracks.

"......I just felt a chill," he muttered.

His sixth sense sent him a warning.

He braced with cleaver and great shield—but nothing attacked.

"...Just my imagination?"

It wasn't. But the actual source was too far away for him to notice.

The third event lasted a week.

By the fifth day, Maple had farmed enough to meet her goal.

"Yes! Counter is mine!"

Hearing that Maple had this skill would make many a player quake in their boots.

But there was nothing they could do to stop it now.

Maple was steadily filling in the gaps of her extremely specialized build.

But her most powerful attacks were growing weaker, as the rest of the player base found means of dealing with potent poison.

Counter would be extra effective against anyone who'd focused too much on that meta.

And obtaining the skill meant she'd accomplished everything she wanted out of this event.

With nothing to gain by hunting more bulls, she stopped focusing her efforts on it.

She just wasn't feeling motivated.

Freed from the bull hunt, Maple was left to her own devices.

Upon hearing that news, quite a few players would likely immediately begin trying to convince her how much fun bull hunting really was.

There was a chance that Maple might well find herself surrounded.

But currently, there were no other players in sight.

"Where do you think we should go, Syrup?"

Syrup never answered, but she talked to it anyway.

Especially when she wasn't sure what to do with herself.

There were rewards based on a guild's collective haul, so she couldn't *completely* stop the hunt, but Sally, Kasumi, and Chrome were well on their way to earning all the points the guild needed.

"Is there anything else I could do? Is there, like, a super-big bull out there?"

Below her was a forest.

She decided to stop looking from the air and jumped down into it.

"This is the place I got the Archangel's Fragment, I think. I still don't know my way around that well..."

Sally had memorized the whole map right away.

Maybe these things came with experience.

Maple might have joined the top-ranked players, but her actual playtime was still total noob tier.

This wasn't a primary bull-hunt zone, so it was awfully quiet.

Maple didn't find much to do beyond taking out the occasional bull as she came across them.

And as she wandered around doing just that, she stumbled across a familiar building.

"Oh, the church!"

She hadn't explored it much before, so she went on in.

Last time, she'd picked up the Archangel's Fragment and rushed off pretty quickly, but this time, she checked every corner of the place.

"It's pretty rundown, but you never know! I might find a book here."

She'd found one in the second event, and it had turned out to be a pretty big clue.

She looked along every wall and under all the pews but with no luck.

"I guess…that's the last place left."

She headed to the floor where she'd found the fragment.

Where the bottle had been…she found tiny red letters.

Unable to read them standing, she got down on her hands and knees, tracing them with her fingers.

"Um…Summon?" she muttered.

The moment she uttered that word, the entire church floor glowed red.

It grew brighter and brighter until the walls and ceilings were dyed red, too.

"Uh-oh!"

Maple jumped up and tried to beat a hasty retreat, but the light was already blinding.

When it finally died down, Maple opened her eyes...

".........Uh...what?"

The interior before her was definitely the same church, but it had all turned...gray.

This was unnerving.

"Where...am I?"

Something was clearly going on here, but if it was gonna take a while, she might have to bail.

That was easy enough—she'd just log out—but there was no guarantee she could get back here.

She'd have to choose wisely.

For now, she decided to turn and head outside.

"Yikes... What a nightmare!"

The exterior was just as relentlessly gray.

No green trees—just a barren gray wasteland as far as the eye could see.

It was like time had stopped—she could see bricks here and there, floating in midair.

"Sally would hate this...," Maple muttered and started walking.

With purpose!

She'd seen one thing out there that *wasn't* gray.

And she was headed toward it.

She reached the non-gray thing...

A pitch-black sphere.

It seemed to respond to her approach—the surface began to bulge.

Then the sphere exploded, and something emerged, dripping fluid black as coal.

A tail snaked out from beneath a tattered robe.

Curly, ram-like horns.

Head still down, it growled, "Dinner's here?"

Maple raised her shield.

Her foe raised its head and saw Maple...

"Mm? You're the one from... I smell the angel's power on you! Fortune smiles on me. We demons earn our ranks by consuming foes like you. You may have beat me at the temple, but here I wield my full power!"

The demon howled.

Diplomacy was not an option.

She would have to fight.

Maple felt no fear. As she steeled herself for combat, she took the demon at its word.

"You want to eat me? Well, I'll eat you right back!"

With that ominous pronouncement, their battle began.

Maple had taken a single step off the third event's path...and found herself on a track leading right to Weirdville.

◆☐◆☐◆☐◆☐◆

The demon charged Maple, ramming her with incredible force.

Unable to react in time, she stood fast as the impact struck her body.

"Cool! No damage."

Once again, her defense had saved her bacon.

However...

"Mm?"

There was a bloodred chain wrapped around her. Clearly a side effect of the demon's attack.

"What is it...?"

As Maple blinked at it, the demon attacked again.

"There I was, possessing a woman with an angel's power...and you had to interfere!"

"Well, yeah! I helped her out! Urp...you're too fast!"

Once again, Maple couldn't dodge in time.

"More chains…?"

She was pretty sure those were bad news, so she decided to add a buffer.

"Wool Up!"

A fluffy white ball appeared in the discolored gray realm.

Maple huddled inside the wool, fleeing the demon's attacks and inspecting the chains.

"If you've inherited the angel's power, then I'll simply have to strip it from you!"

"Hmph! Nothing scares me in here! Um…Cursebind? I've never heard of that status effect."

She read through the details.

It could stack up to five times, and if it did, that would lower all stats by 25 percent.

"I'm at two stacks, which means I'm down ten percent."

Cursebind would lose a stack after two minutes, so she'd have to wait four whole minutes to be ailment-free again.

"In that case, I'll stay in here!"

She waited inside her fluff until the bind was gone, then popped her head out of the wool, released Syrup, and had it fly.

"Giganticize!"

Once Syrup was ten yards overhead, she had it point its head diagonally down.

Making sure the demon was attacking her wool, she gave the order.

"Spirit Cannon!"

A massive laser beam hurtled down from the skies above.

From far too high for her enemy to reach.

It scorched the earth, swallowing up the demon.

"Man, this is one tough customer… That only took away ten percent of its health!"

Apparently, the demon wasn't exaggerating about having access to its full power here; the damage it had sustained didn't even slow it down. In fact, it seemed to be hitting harder and faster.

Maple hadn't fought many enemies who could survive more than a couple hits from her—a record few great shielders could boast of. She'd done "only 10 percent damage," but by the standards of anyone else in her weapon class, that was plenty impressive. (She remained unaware of this fact.)

She ducked back into her wool shelter, thinking.

"Maybe I could just poke my arm out and use Hydra? But I feel like poison wouldn't work very well on a demon."

And if she poisoned the wool, Syrup wouldn't be able to pick her up, and she'd be stuck here.

Wanting to avoid that fate, she was being extremely conservative about poison use.

She poked her head and New Moon out of one side, waiting for the demon.

The demon punched her in the face, but Maple's head was so hard, even swords bounced off it.

No way a bare fist could do any damage.

"Hydra!"

A poison dragon shot out of New Moon, swallowing up the demon.

"Yeah, poison doesn't work."

It might not apply to the DOT effect, but Hydra's attack itself did do damage.

That was better than nothing, but not particularly efficient.

"I'll leave this one to Syrup."

With Cursebind in effect once again, she ducked back into the safety of her wool—just in case.

She ordered laser support fire every few minutes until the demon was nearly down to half health.

"Spirit Cannon!"

The demon was swallowed up in Syrup's beam once more.

And its remaining health finally dipped below the 50 percent mark.

"Gah… Enough! I must crush you… *Crush you!*"

The demon's body was suddenly wreathed in black light. It began to swell.

Its limbs grew massive, muscles bulging—and increasing in number.

Its neck extended, its face fading until all that remained was a gaping, drooling maw.

Newly hideous, the black demon roared.

"Grrr…grrraghhhh!"

"G-gross!"

Maple did not have it in her to like anything that looked like *this*.

"Grrrr…arghhhh!"

Jet-black flames emerged from its maw.

They enveloped Maple, setting her wool alight.

"Huh? My wool is flammable?!"

Wool generally was. No matter how high the defense, the material's fundamental properties didn't change.

As the wool wall defending her quickly burned away, Maple fell to the ground.

The demon came at her, maw yawning wide.

"Raghhh!"

"Oh…"

And it swallowed Maple whole.

Her shield and sword fell to the ground.

"Grrraaaaagghhhhhha-ha-ha-ha!"

Crowing over its victory, the demon let out a heinous cackle.

*   *   *

Maple found herself sliding down a slimy passage.

"Ugh...so cramped! Augh!"

She was suddenly released—and fell, landing in a pool.

Trying not to drown, she grabbed on to something nearby.

"Ew...am I inside its stomach? My armor's melting!"

She started to panic but soon realized that *she* wasn't dissolving, so she calmed down enough to examine her surroundings.

"Hmm," Maple muttered. "No way to fight back. No, wait, there is!"

Whoever had designed this boss had set the "swallow" attack to deal a pretty high amount of damage.

And once inside, the constriction did a *lot* more damage, eventually dropping players in this pool of poison.

Every now and then, the stomach walls constricted, so if you survived the poison, you'd be crushed to death.

Notoriously slow, great shielders would normally have to fend off the nimble demon's swallow attacks with technique alone.

But Maple had punched right through all these challenges with raw VIT and Poison Nullification.

She'd soaked enough damage to kill three regular great shielders, then fell in a pool of almost certain death with no more concern than if it was lukewarm water.

As baths went, it was on the cold side.

And in this final destination, where nobody was expected to survive, Maple's armor was melting...and getting stronger.

"It ate me...but if I beat it, can I get out?"

Maple began swimming across the poison lake toward the pulsating walls.

An hour after Maple got eaten…

The demon's HP bar was dropping steadily.

This was changing up its attack patterns, but these attacks had no enemies to hit.

Because she was inside it.

"How far am I? *Munch, munch.* Is its health getting low yet?"

Maple took another bite out of the fleshy wall.

The short sword Iz had made for her to use in angel form had been quickly running out of durability, so she abandoned her plans to attack with it.

And Syrup was back in the ring…leaving this her only means of attack.

"It's really thrashing around…"

Maple was being peeled off the wall and tossed around by the sheer force, but she was steadily gnawing away at her foe's HP.

Another hour later…

Maple finally consumed the demon's life.

Its body turned to light and scattered—dropping Maple unceremoniously to the ground.

"Oof…whew! Finally made it."

Maple picked up her great shield and short sword, and an alert popped up.

"I thought I might get Demon Eater, but…since I have Martyr's Devotion…"

Martyr's Devotion was a prerequisite for the actual new skill.

Plus, it would offer her another offensive tactic to add to her repertoire.

"Saturating Chaos… This is…hmm, fascinating. Feels a lot like Hydra. Should be easy for me to use!"

This skill came with three sub-skills.

After a thorough examination, Maple wasted no time setting it on her armor. No reason not to take advantage of her empty slots.

"Okay...let's head back and try it out!"

As she spoke, her vision was bathed in red light...and once it vanished, she was back in the church.

"This one has no MP cost, so let's give this a whirl! Uh...Predators!" Maple cried.

A pitch-black light appeared at her feet, and two black *things* reached out of it.

Each three yards long.

They looked a lot like the demon had, post-transformation.

There was a huge maw on one end, but unlike the demon, these protrusions had no limbs—these snakelike growths came directly from the ground.

"Can they move...?"

When Maple stepped forward, the Predators followed, glowing lights and all.

"In that case, we're outta here!"

Maple emerged from the church.

She had gone into an old church and come out with newborn demons at her side.

And she didn't walk far before she learned something valuable.

"Oh! If we encounter monsters, they'll beat them for me!"

Anything that got close enough for the Predators to reach was swiftly rent asunder.

And their HP, attack, and defense values were all independent of Maple's, so their DPS was rock-solid.

On top of all that, their attacks applied Cursebind.

"Okay...now let's try a skill that takes MP. Saturating Chaos!"

Activating this skill generated a dark light inside Maple herself, and when it hit the saturation point, it attacked to the fore—like Hydra but shaped like a giant version of the Predators flanking her.

If she'd been fighting another player, and the poor victim had soaked this attack head-on, they'd have been gobbled up by a gaping maw over two yards wide.

Solid range, too.

"And last… No, let's save that for later. Uh, Seal!"

This command returned the Predators to the darkness from whence they came. She'd gained one more new skill but was in no rush to try it—instead, she exited the forest.

"Hmm, the third event's still ongoing, but…I dunno…maybe I'm done?"

She'd lost all interest in it, and ultimately added only a handful of bulls to her score before it ended.

The event wrapped up without Maple doing anything else remarkable.

And once it was over, the members of Maple Tree all gathered in the Guild Home.

"Whew…I'm beat," Sally said, wearily flopping into a chair. She looked thoroughly exhausted.

"Same here." Kasumi echoed the sentiment, not bothering to lift her head off the table.

They'd taken out more bulls than anyone and had earned some rest.

Below them came Chrome and then Kanade.

Maple, meanwhile, was not remotely tired.

She'd earned less points than anyone (excepting Iz) and spent the tail end of the event in a secluded forest using Predators to do all the work for her—in other words, she hadn't done anything that might wear her out.

"You didn't do much this time, huh, Maple?"

"Just...couldn't stay motivated."

"Can't blame you. This event was stacked against players like us," Chrome grumbled.

The structure of the bull hunt really rewarded those with high AGI stats.

And Maple was the opposite of that.

"But we got to the top-ranked guild reward!"

Kanade was right—the other four had more than made up for Maple's shortcomings, and the event was a resounding success.

"It's already here!" Iz said, taking out the reward.

It was a stuffed bull's head, a displayable item that could be used to decorate the Guild Home wall.

And it gave every member of Maple Tree a 3 percent boost to STR.

"And that stacks!"

"So it seems."

"But it does *nothing* for me... Oh, wait, actually, it does!" Maple said.

Everyone but Kanade immediately looked concerned.

Maple's STR was a big fat 0, so this percentage boost really shouldn't have mattered to her.

If it did, there was only one reason.

"Maple...where exactly were you during this event?"

"I was on the second stratum...mostly."

She wasn't sure if that gray world counted.

Sally and Kasumi both put a hand to their brow in consternation.

Chrome and Iz realized their efforts to stop her had been in vain.

".........They're opening a third stratum soon. You'll have to show us what you were up to when we're clearing the dungeon to gain access."

Everyone present had concluded that Maple *must* have done something nuts. Whatever new skill she had acquired was definitely not ordinary.

This was a fair assumption.

But the skill in question was neither Predators nor Saturating Chaos—it was the remaining skill, the one even Maple had hesitated to try.

Only three days to go before the launch of the third stratum.

◆□◆□◆□◆□◆

Not long after the launch, Maple Tree was busy blazing a path through the dungeon leading to the new stratum.

All six of them, Iz included.

The game's maximum party size was eight, so at the current guild head count, they could all be in the same party.

And this party could clear any current dungeon the game could throw at it.

So far, Sally, Chrome, and Kasumi—backed up by Kanade's support spells—had easily handled everything they had encountered.

Maple had not joined a single fight. She'd spent her time guarding Iz instead.

"Okay! Boss room!"

"Let's take this thing down!"

"Ready when you are."

Kasumi opened the door, and they all stepped in.

The boss loomed in the depths.

It was a giant tree with a face on the trunk.

The first-stratum boss had also been vegetal, and the fruit on its trees had been generating a barrier, so everyone immediately scanned this new boss for any sort of fruit or nut—but they found none.

"Let me go first," Maple said. "Taunt!"

Maple started walking toward the boss.

It was attacking with roots and branches, but these had absolutely no effect on her.

She reached the base of its trunk in no time.

"Predators! Hydra! Saturating Chaos!"

Monsters spawned on either side of her, Hydra poisoned the trunk, and finally the gaping maws ripped off a chunk of the boss.

Its HP plummeted.

The two Predators were still attacking. In boss fights, there was no reason to hold back on any skills, no matter how high the cost.

The tree boss grew enraged, focusing its attacks on the two Predators.

"Martyr's Devotion!"

Maple's HP took a hit as her angel wings unfurled. Maple was now negating all the damage the Predators took.

She quickly chugged a potion, restoring her health.

The rest of her party was watching the battle unfold from the doorway.

"What... What are those? Those are *clearly* monsters. *She's* a monster."

"Yeah...can't argue with that."

"How does she manage to get more crazy things every time I see her?"

"It's a relief to know she's still being Maple."

"Yeah, as long as she's on our side..."

Each of them was doing their best to process Maple's latest evolution.

But Maple still had one skill left to show.

And she'd made up her mind to try it out here—so this fight wasn't over till she did.

"Let's do it... Atrocity."

With that soft whisper, Maple's body was enveloped in a sinister glimmer.

Then a pitch-black column of light shot toward the ceiling, and suddenly Maple...closely resembled the two monsters flanking her.

There was one big difference—she had an array of limbs.

And as her form changed, the Predators vanished.

This new monster charged the tree boss, latching on to it and breathing fire.

The flames were highly effective against wood, and the boss tried to fight back with every root, branch, and spell it could muster.

But not only did it fail to beat this demon, it couldn't even leave a scratch.

The monster's claws tore the trunk apart wholesale. Its kicks left craters in the bark. The gaping jaws violently ripped away chunks of wood.

The ferocious struggle went on like this for a short while, but the tree boss never stood a chance and was soon defeated.

The monster turned and walked toward the rest of the party.

As they braced themselves, its maw yawned open.

"Man, this is hard to control!" the monster squeaked.

All five brains short-circuited.

"M-Maple?"

"Yep! It's me!"

There was a distortion effect, but the voice was clearly Maple's.

As they stared in horror, Sally asked the big question. "Can you switch back?"

"Hmm. Lemme see."

A few minutes later, cracks appeared on the monster's belly, and Maple fell out.

Once she was free, the monster shell she had emerged from disintegrated.

Dusting herself off, Maple trotted back to her friends.

"I'd appreciate some form of explanation. Honestly, whatever you can tell us…," Sally said.

This one was clearly beyond even her.

"Uh…so that thing cancels all equipment effects but raises STR and AGI by 50 each, gives me 1,000 HP, and if I run out of HP, it just puts me back in my regular body."

The main downside was losing access to equipment stat boosts and skills. There was also a once-per-day use limit.

But if Maple was ever in real danger, this skill could serve as a useful last resort.

"Uh…so you've *literally* become inhuman at long last."

"Yes. Not a trace of humanity left. That much is obvious."

Maple had always been a monster, but that was no longer a metaphor.

"It's hard to move in, though… I guess it's like wearing a really big mascot costume?"

In that form, she wasn't capable of finesse.

"And, uh…things were plenty weird before you transformed."

By the time the twin Predators had spawned, Sally had already been gaping in horror. "Even I can tell that you've seriously entered crazy territory."

"Hmm... Also, it's faster than riding Syrup!"

"I have to say that it would probably be unwise to use it to travel," Kanade said gravely.

That was less *girl hitting the road with her monster pals* and more *nightmarish fiend running amok.*

"If you want to practice fighting in that form, please do so deep in the mountains."

"Anyone who sees it will get the wrong idea..."

No reason not to use a skill once learned.

Maple turned and headed toward the third stratum, and the others followed.

Clouds loomed above the third stratum; the main town's theme was machines and tools.

As the members of Maple Tree stepped onto the third floor, they all noticed one thing—

Every player who came here noticed the same thing.

"They're all flying!" Maple gasped.

The air was filled with players riding all manner of machinery.

"Some sort of item?"

"Hmm...probably that."

Sally was pointing at the market ahead, where gold could be exchanged for all sorts of devices. As they watched, a player made a purchase, then hefted an inscrutable gizmo onto his back. As soon as he did, it started glowing blue and sent him rocketing off into the skies above.

"This stratum is certainly different."

"You can say that again. Guess we all get to fly this time."

Once they'd processed what passed for normal here, they headed toward their third-stratum Guild Home.

CHAPTER 5

Defense Build and Recruiting

Inside their new Guild Home, they scoped out the interior.

Once they'd gotten a handle on the layout, they all gathered in the main room.

"Yo, Maple! I got a topic to discuss."

"What is it, Chrome?"

"Just got a message from the admins. It's a ways off yet, but they're warning us to get ready for a guild versus guild combat event. And…"

"And what?"

"They're compressing time again. On the off chance one of us can't make it, we might wanna up our membership numbers…or at least consider the idea."

Chrome raised a fair point. As is, there were only six members, and Iz was a noncombatant.

If anyone had to sit out, the event would undoubtedly become much harder.

"Hmm… Fair enough. I'm down for that."

Maple gave her seal of approval.

The downsides of having so few members were clear and apparent, even to her.

"I know a few people I could ask, but...I think this one's best left to the guild master."

The "people" Chrome mentioned included the other members of the Maple watchers forum, but this wasn't his guild, and he wasn't about to insist on the idea.

"In that case," Sally started saying as she clapped a hand on Maple's shoulders, "wanna go scouting with me tomorrow?"

"Hmm...Okay! Let's do that."

The two of them set "find new members" as their daily goal.

And the next day found them roaming the streets, looking for potential recruits.

"But how do we find people?"

"Let's check the board. That usually has all sorts of postings, including guild and party hopefuls."

"Sounds good to me!"

Maple followed Sally's lead, heading to the board in question.

Once they arrived, Maple skimmed the posts. The newer listings had lots of DPS BUILD and POISON RESIST REQUIRED.

"Offensive builds are popular, huh? They must be fun!"

"...You could say that, yeah."

Sally looked the board over herself, but anyone capable of being instantly useful wouldn't be looking for a party here in the first place.

"Hmm, no standouts, huh? Just low-level players still stuck on the first stratum."

Sally turned away from the board, so Maple followed her lead.

"Should we head to the first stratum, then? Will that help?" Maple suggested.

Sally thought the odds of them finding anyone useful down there were low, but it was better than nothing.

"Sure, why not?" she said. "It's better than standing here staring at posts, at least."

They'd only just reached the third stratum but were already headed back to the first.

Neither had been down here in a while, and as they walked, Maple noticed something odd.

"There are a lot more…slow walkers around."

Everywhere she looked, there were people plodding along.

"Probably people copying you, Maple. They must be doing extreme builds."

"Huh? R-really?"

"And a lot of them will end up starting over with new accounts."

Sally knew exactly how these trends went.

Maple didn't, so this news came as a huge shock.

"Huh? Why?!"

"They can't dodge, but their HP is low, and…there're lots of downsides. The biggest issue is that they start to realize how many things an extreme build can't do—like find guilds or parties. It kills half the fun!"

Maple was the only player who'd managed to make a truly extreme build work.

And nobody could copy what she'd done so easily, which naturally meant none of her copycats was going to get far.

"Now I'm feeling guilty…"

"No need! Everyone looks up to the best players. This just happens to be a case where it backfired on 'em."

"Okay…I'll try not to worry, then."

"Oh…I guess we could at least post something saying we've got openings."

"Good point. Let's do that."

Sally was more experienced at handling these things, so she sped off toward the noticeboard.

Left to her own devices, Maple settled down on an empty bench and waited for Sally to get back.

"Hmm... People copying me, huh?"

That idea was still bugging her.

So when two nearby players started talking about the problems it caused, she couldn't help but listen in.

"Aw...another party said no. I guess extreme builds really aren't good."

"Cheer up! We haven't played that long yet. Plus, we can always start over if it really doesn't work out!"

"But then..."

The voices were on her right, so Maple turned to look.

She saw two girls talking and decided to approach.

"Hello!" she said. "Um...do you mind if I interrupt?"

Both heads swiveled.

They were not only the same height—their faces and weapons were identical, too. Anyone who saw them would instantly assume they were twins.

The sole difference was that the encouraging player had white hair, while the discouraged player had black hair.

The white-haired one was the first to respond. "Er... Wh-what is it?"

"Well, um..."

Maple wasn't sure what to say. Or even why she'd called out to them, really. She just didn't want to hear players lamenting their extreme builds.

"We're kinda busy here..."

"Oh, um...r-right! My party—er, guild! Wanna join?"

"...Huh? I mean...thanks for the offer, but...you're super high level, right? Your gear is obviously... Are you sure?"

These girls were almost entirely in starting gear and were clearly feeling inadequate.

"Totally! I'm the guild master, and we've got plenty of room for more!"

Technically, she was the authority when it came to adding new members.

Nobody in Maple Tree would object if she brought in these two.

"Maple, I'm ba— Oh, new faces?"

"Oh, there you are, Sally! I was just recruiting them!"

"Aha... Well, if you want 'em, I'm down. And nobody you pick would ever be normal, so..."

"Huh? R-really?"

"Yup. Let's hit up the first-stratum Guild Home and talk there!"

"Good idea. Will you two follow us?"

""O-okay...""

Maple and Sally led the way as the two girls followed with some trepidation.

They'd been about to give up when a hand reached down from heaven.

And that hand belonged to the sole example of a successful extreme build.

◆□◆□◆□◆□◆

The four of them were sitting around a table in the Guild Home, talking things over.

On the way, Sally had dashed back to the board to remove the recruitment post, so for now, they wouldn't be adding anyone else.

Discussions like this were more Sally's thing than Maple's, so she was handling answering the bulk of the questions.

The girl with white hair was named Yui, and the one with black hair was named Mai.

They were both level 4 and had yet to learn any skills.

Both were wielding hammers—huge ones that were one and a half times their own heights.

"So you mentioned you're both doing extreme builds?" Maple asked.

"Yes! We've both put all our points in STR."

The reason for this was that in real life, neither was known for her strength or endurance—so in-game, they wanted to pour everything into their characters' strength.

"Huh...that's a lot like you, Maple."

"Ah-ha-ha...true."

Like them, Maple hadn't been too concerned about in-game advantages or disadvantages.

And since neither of them had recognized her, copying Maple clearly wasn't one of their motivations.

"So...you're also an extreme build?"

"Yep, I am! I put everything in VIT!"

They both looked surprised.

Neither had come across any player who'd made this work before.

"Yeah, well...Maple's not exactly a useful role model."

Maple couldn't argue with that.

"Well, Sally? Can we add them?"

"Sure, no prob. Pure STR builds don't have much downside with you around... If we can get them leveled in a month, it should all work out."

With Sally on board, Yui and Mai were officially in.

Maple registered both of them as the newest members of the Maple Tree guild.

Next order of business was to get them to the third stratum, where Maple Tree was currently operating.

"Do you have time today?"

"Er, um, yes. We do. Right?"

"Yeah, I have time."

"Then Maple and I will run you straight up to stratum three."

""Y-you will?!""

They were still gaping even as they headed out of town.

Once they were outside of town, Sally turned around and said, "Maple, the usual, please."

"Roger!"

Maple summoned Syrup as requested and had everyone hop aboard before taking flight. The two girls were understandably shocked from start to finish.

"Keep your hands and feet inside the ride at all times, okay?"

With that playful warning from Maple, those shocked expressions simply became dumbfounded.

"Trust me—this is only the beginning... Better to start getting used to it now."

Sally was already thinking about the future. Even after setting Maple aside, the Maple Tree guild was an assembly of mind-blowing talent and skill. If they could get used to Maple, they would be able to get used to anyone.

All future recruits would have to undergo the same conditioning if they wanted to last in Maple Tree.

Having made swift work of the dungeon, they stepped through the doors to the boss room—beyond this lay the second stratum.

"Aaah… Sorry in advance if we die," Mai moaned. She seemed really worried about inconveniencing them.

"Oh…that won't happen. Trust me."

"Martyr's Devotion!"

Maple's hair changed color, and her angel wings unfurled.

The twins instantly froze.

This was beyond comprehension.

"I'll handle this one. Have a seat right here!"

"Gotcha! Make it a good one!"

Maple moved the twins out of the way.

"………! A-are you sure? Sally's on her own! Against a b-boss?!" Yui said, grabbing Maple's hand.

"Yeah, she's got this. I've never seen Sally take damage."

""…………What?""

"Look, she's starting."

Maple pointed up ahead. Sally had summoned Oboro and was racing toward the deer.

Attacks she'd already seen were nothing to Sally; she was twisting and ducking and dodging everything, never breaking stride.

"Oboro! Shadow Clone!"

At her command, there were suddenly five Sallys, all taking different paths toward the boss deer.

This shocked even Maple.

"Since when can Oboro do *that*?"

"S-Sally's incredible! H-how can she dodge like that? And she can clone herself?!" Yui was getting quite worked up.

"Apparently…? This one's new to me, too…"

Meanwhile, the aura that buffed Sally's attack was getting bigger.

Between her magic and dagger strikes and Oboro's fire, the deer was downed in a little over ten minutes.

When the fight was done, Sally trotted back to them.

"Oboro's getting so strong!"

"Yup. Let's go take out the second-stratum boss!"

They quickly reached the second stratum and immediately dived right into the next dungeon.

"I ain't fighting this one."

"Mm, got it."

Maple was gonna go solo against the second-stratum boss.

Yui and Mai gave Sally anxious looks.

After all, Maple was a great shielder, and all they knew was that she'd sunk all her points into VIT.

Martyr's Devotion had proven how strong her defense was, but they hadn't seen Maple fight at all, so there was no reason to believe she was good at it.

Oblivious to their concern, Maple opened the door and stepped into the boss room.

"Are you sure you shouldn't help her, Sally?"

"I—I really think you should!"

"Heh. That's a new one…"

This may have been the first time Sally saw anyone worry about Maple.

Which spoke to just how universally recognized Maple was—as a threat.

"You thought I was impressive?"

""Er…y-yes, very.""

Inhuman reflexes. Powerful skills.

Her battle with the deer went well past "impressive."

"You're about to see a battle not of this world that defies all logic."

She made sure they were paying attention, then turned to watch Maple head in herself.

The twins might not get it now, but in a few scant seconds, it would all fall into place.

"Sally said to strut my stuff, so… Syrup!"
She made Syrup size up and fly.
The boss was attacking her the whole time but did no damage.
"Hydra! Saturating Chaos! Syrup, Spirit Cannon!"
The boss was hit by a three-headed poison dragon, a spectral maw, and a blinding laser beam all at once.
While it was busy reeling from the attack, Maple moved closer, negating all its damage, and swung her great shield.
Devour left a deep gouge in the boss's trunk. This flurry of powerful moves made the boss's health plummet like a rock.
And Maple wasn't done yet.
"Predators! Martyr's Devotion!"
Monsters appeared on either side of her and immediately latched on to the boss with their jaws.
Maple unfurled her angel wings, protecting them.
The boss screamed, renewing its attacks on Maple and her minions with branches and magic, but to no avail.
"Atrocity!"
Black light poured out of her, coalescing into a giant monster form.
She breathed fire, gnashed her sharp jaws, and tore away chunks of the boss.
A one-sided butchering. It was no longer clear which of them was the actual boss.

"Whew…all done!"
"Maple, change back to your real form."
"Oh, sorry, sorry."

Maple fell out of the monster's belly, and it vanished.

"Let's hit the third stratum!"

"Sure."

Maple turned and headed off.

Sally looked back at Yui and Mai.

"She's the best we got. See? I'm *normal*."

""………………"""

They both stood rooted to the spot, jaws hanging open, their brains utterly unable to process what they'd just seen.

"But you two have a lot in common with her. You guys might just end up like that someday!"

Sally took their hands and pulled them toward the third stratum.

CHAPTER 6

Defense Build and Powering Up

When they reached the third-stratum Guild Home, Maple cheerily introduced Yui and Mai to the rest of the crew.

Then the two of them elected to log out for the day.

"You've both leveled up a little, but you'll need a lot more... Hmm. Maple, when can the three of you play together next?"

The girls compared notes, aligning their schedules.

"Maple, lend me your ear."

"Mm? What, what?"

Sally whispered something to her.

".........Okay!"

"I'll take care of the prep."

"Cool, got it."

The twins looked puzzled, but for now, everyone was dismissed.

On the appointed day, the three of them were together once more. Sally had gifts for the twins.

"Take these," she said, handing them headgear that covered their heads completely, making it impossible to see their faces. "Use these and follow Maple's instructions."

Both girls nodded.

"All right! Follow me!"

""A-aye-aye!""

They trailed out of the Guild Home after Maple. Sally had some business of her own to take care of, so she wasn't logging out just yet.

"You going, too, Chrome?"

He'd been heading out the door himself—but not to help Maple.

"Yeah...Kasumi's already at it."

It was currently summer. And all summer long, monsters had a low chance of dropping watermelons.

Collecting these would enhance the guild's support effects.

That meant stat boosts. These watermelons could raise STR, AGI, and INT by a maximum of 10 points each. Just as gathering enough dirt makes a mountain, making sure to hit that quota every time would amount to a substantial permanent boost to all guild members.

"I've got Maple handling the twins' power leveling, so securing the guild buffs is on us."

"Lords knows what they'll come back as... They're not out hunting a unique series, are they?"

"Nah, just getting some levels for now. Somewhere on the first stratum, away from prying eyes..."

There was a reason they were trying to avoid attention.

When she explained this to Chrome, he made a face and nodded.

Meanwhile, Maple had brought the twins to a deserted corner of the first stratum.

They were outside the dungeon where she'd fought the hydra.

"Are we running this dungeon?"

"Yep, we are! Put those things on!"

The twins equipped their helmets.

With their faces covered like this, nobody could tell who they were.

"Martyr's Devotion!"

Maple went right into angel form, hair glimmering gold in a glow of divine light.

They'd seen this before so were able to admire the beauty of it without reeling in surprise.

"Atrocity!"

But that feeling did not last long.

Maple swiftly transformed into a hideous beast. Only the effects of Martyr's Devotion remained. Even her wings were gone.

"Hop on! Oh, make sure you get at least one hit in on the boss."

These two girls were really strong…so they could easily hold on to the creature Maple had become.

"Oh, and if anyone sees us, I'm gonna pretend to be a monster, okay?"

Their heads were hidden, so nobody could match their faces to their guild and their guild to Maple; this whole rigamarole was purely to prevent anyone from realizing who monster-form-Maple really was.

They wanted to keep that ace up their sleeve until the guild event.

""Huh?""

"Grah! Grrrrr!" Maple said and flung herself down the cave.

There was no need to role-play *now*, but she felt like it.

She shredded every monster along the way, opened the door to the boss room, and charged right at the hydra waiting within.

The poor hydra fell once more to her voracious appetite.

Yui and Mai had each landed a blow before its demise, so they leveled up.

And then came the important step.

Unlike the last time, two magic circles appeared before them.

One led to town—the other to the dungeon entrance.

Sally had explained that after clearing a dungeon once, subsequent runs would offer up this second circle.

And Maple took the new circle back to the entrance.

If they left the dungeon, the boss would respawn.

Their reason for coming here was to farm the hydra boss.

This poison dragon was far and away the toughest foe on the first stratum.

And it took an awfully long trip from town to get here, so with the current boom in extreme builds, not many players were inclined to make the arduous hike.

Best of all, the dungeon itself was quite short.

They could clear the deserted dungeon in a flash, rip the rotting dragon to shreds, and then consume it piece by piece.

And as they repeated this process, the twins rapidly leveled up.

Maple knew the route by heart, so she never got lost, and there was nothing around that could challenge her onslaught.

Maple was looping the dungeon at astonishing speeds, averaging just over three minutes per run.

After checking her time a few runs in, she felt an urge.

Yes...

She wanted to crack the sub-three range.

There was no real meaning to this. All she had to do was be a few seconds faster.

Maple was beginning to discover the fun that could be had when repeating the same run over and over again.

Taking this corner a little tighter, slaughtering all the monsters at that spot with fire breath before they clashed, avoiding anything that might slow her down...

Opening the boss door with no wasted motion, hitting the boss itself as hard as she could.

A few attempts after she started consciously working at it, her time dipped below the three-minute mark.

She felt like there was still room for improvement.

She could beat that hydra faster.

If she had Yui and Mai go all out on it, they could make some real gains.

After several tries doing that...

Yui's and Mai's new levels were boosting their attack strength, and they actually shaved down their run time to under 2:30.

"Yesssss!" Maple roared, her voice all staticky.

There was no reward for this, but Maple felt a great sense of accomplishment.

""Maple! Maple!""

"Mm? What?"

""Look!""

The twins showed Maple their stat screens.

Her head had no eyes, but for some reason, she could still see just fine.

"Um...Annihilator? And Conqueror?"

"Let me see... Conqueror is for beating a boss a bunch under a certain time limit. Prereq is a lot of STR. And we got Annihilator because of the dungeon speedrun. You need a lot of STR for that, too."

Maple's Atrocity had boosted her stats, but those numbers weren't real, so there was no way for her to get these skills.

The twins showed her the full skill listing, and Maple noticed something interesting.

Conqueror

Doubles the user's STR. Costs 3x the points to raise VIT, AGI, or INT.

Condition

Defeat a boss a set number of times under a set time limit. Requires STR: 100+.

Specifically, this Conqueror skill was the STR version of her Absolute Defense.

"Hmm... Don't think Kasumi would need that. Or Chrome... and Sally would hate the downside..."

The guild members with DPS builds were all raising several stats, so they wouldn't want a skill that stunted their growth in all but one area.

"And Annihilator...is *really* good."

Annihilator

Allows one-handed use of two-handed weapons.

Condition

Clear a dungeon below a set time limit. Requires STR: 100+.

In other words, they could now dual-wield giant hammers like Sally did daggers.

"How about we do a few more loops and then head home?"
""Okay!""

◆□◆□◆□◆□◆

After countless loops of the hydra dungeon, they finally called it a day.

Yui and Mai climbed down off Maple's back, and she reverted to her human form.

"Whew," she said, stretching. "I'm all worn out! That was fun, though."

"Oh, um. Maple, thank you so much! We gained so many levels!"

Yui turned and bowed. Mai followed suit, thanking her, too.

"Mm, great! But I hear there are some really high-level players out there. I'm still on the low end! Sally said the highest player is… sixty-one now?"

"S-sixty-one?! Th-that's…mind-blowing."

"What level are you now, Mai?"

Recovering quickly from their surprise, the twins turned to assessing the results of the day's grind.

"Probably the same as you, Yui. Um…twenty."

Mai was clearly still not used to opening her status menu, but she managed after a moment and showed it to her sister.

Yui opened her own for comparison and then had an idea.

"Oh! Should we let Maple look over our stats? Do you mind, Mai?"

"Hmm. I'd say…yeah, let's do that." Mai said, nodding.

They took a step toward Maple and showed her their stat blocks.

Mai

Lv20   HP 35/35   MP 20/20

[STR 160 <+25>]   [VIT 0]
[AGI 0]   [DEX 0]
[INT 0]

Equipment

Head	[None]		Body	[None]
R. Hand	[Iron Hammer]		L. Hand	[Iron Hammer]
Legs	[None]		Feet	[None]
Accessories	[None]			
	[None]			
	[None]			

Skills

Conqueror, Annihilator

Yui

Lv20   HP 35/35   MP 20/20

[STR 160 <+25>]   [VIT 0]
[AGI 0]   [DEX 0]
[INT 0]

Equipment

Head	[None]	Body	[None]
R. Hand	[Iron Hammer]	L. Hand	[Iron Hammer]
Legs	[None]	Feet	[None]
Accessories	[None]		
	[None]		
	[None]		

Skills

Conqueror, Annihilator

The two girls looked the same, and so did their stat blocks.

"Oh, so the reason you didn't use any skills in combat is because you didn't have any."

"Yes… Everything we fought on our own just killed us before we could land any hits, so we couldn't make enough money to buy any scrolls."

"And it's hard for us to learn skills from beating monsters. That's why we were looking for a guild…"

Most monsters were on the agile side.

Unless you were Maple and just sprayed down the whole area with poison, you'd need to be able to handle a few incoming attacks at the very least.

Maple didn't need to pay those any attention, so she welcomed incoming monsters, but the twins had found that approach didn't work out so well.

"Even if we just head out to gather items, we can't run from any monsters and would wind up dying that way, too…"

"That's why we were thinking about starting over when you called out to us."

They'd also upgraded their weapons before buying some other essentials, which had only dug them in deeper. Without anyone to help, they'd been out of options—but meeting Maple had changed all that.

They were now strong enough to make progress despite the serious drawbacks of their extreme builds.

"Now we just need to have Iz make you some gear. Oh, hang on…"

Maple popped up her screen and switched to the equipment menu.

Then she swapped out her gear for the white set Iz had made for her.

"I had her craft all of this for me recently! And there's the shield she made before that. She's great! You should try asking her for help."

"Can we? I mean…we don't have money," Mai said, checking her cash and even the materials in her inventory.

They had a lot more materials than they'd ever had before, but even still, there seemed little chance they could afford anything as fancy as what Maple had equipped.

Yui looked downcast, clearly thinking the same thing.

But Maple just beamed back at them.

"Totally, totally! I had her make stuff for me when I was broke! And if you need anything, I can help you get it. Sally and I are happy to lend a hand!"

Generosity had been instrumental in getting White Snow made.

"Heh-heh-heh…there's so much left to do! But for now, let's head back to the third-stratum Guild Home. We gotta talk about your gear!"

Maple was acting like a real leader, and the twins were happy to follow.

"We need to tell the others about our new skills!"

"Those should make you instantly viable in any fight."

"That…would be very nice."

Chattering away, they headed home—careful to avoid crowds.

When they arrived back at the Guild Home, they found Kasumi and Sally chatting.

They broke off as Maple's group approached.

"Welcome back. How'd it go? They get some levels?"

"You betcha! They're still not super high level, but they're a lot higher than before!"

"Well, we have time. Getting them third-stratum ready in a single go was always a long shot."

Maple explained that the twins were level 20 now, and Kasumi and Sally were suitably impressed.

As Maple was asking what skills they should have the twins learn, Yui stepped up.

When everyone looked, she said, "U-um! We learned these two skills today."

"Let's see…"

"Can I have a look?"

Kasumi and Sally examined Yui's skills. The ones Maple had accidentally earned them were powerful and would certainly have a huge impact on the direction their builds took.

"Ooo…kay. Right. Thanks for sharing."

"Same here."

They turned away from Yui and stared right at Maple.

"Huh? Wh-what?"

"I dunno if it's what I expected or…worse."

"You always surpass my wildest expectations."

"At the very least, if they've both got those skills, we'll have to rethink things."

Sally had been assuming the twins wouldn't really be much use in a fight for a while yet, but Maple had found a way to make them instantly combat capable.

"Okay, so…Annihilator? If nothing else, we've gotta prep gear that takes advantage of that."

"Oh! Right, right. That's what we came here to talk about!"

"Iz is in the back. I'll go get her."

Kasumi dashed off and returned a minute later, Iz in tow.

"Uh, hi. Yui and Mai, was it?"

""That's right!""

"Um, can I have a look at these skills?"

They showed Iz their screens. Stat points all poured into more attack and two support skills designed to support that build.

Iz read the Annihilator description, nodding.

"Interesting. Well, to get you started— I mean, nobody in our guild can use 'em."

Iz took four hammers out of her inventory and handed two to each twin.

"You can have these," she said. "They'll help for now. These hammers should make it easier for you to land hits, too."

Yui and Mai scoped out their new weapons.

Crystal Hammer
[STR +25] [Supersize]

Supersize
Increase target size.
Effect lasts thirty seconds, with a one-minute cooldown.

---

*　　*　　*

In other words, this skill allowed them to supersize the hammer heads, making it harder to miss.

With their damage output, as long as they hit, the blows would be fatal for most enemies, so this skill was ideal.

"Um, a-are you sure?"

"I mean…these are really nice!"

"Not a problem. They're good, but nobody else in our guild can use 'em, so they were just collecting dust. And…"

""And…?""

"I'll make you something better. We should talk deets."

Iz was being so generous, it clearly made the twins feel guilty, and they were already shooting each other anxious looks.

"Seriously, don't worry about it. Consider it an investment. In return, just think about what you can do for us later."

That finally clinched it for them, and they nodded.

""All right! I'm sure we can help out now!""

"Heh-heh. Then let's figure out what designs you'd like. Come on in to the back, and we'll get your gear sorted out."

Iz headed toward her workshop.

"Er, thank you, everyone!"

"We'll do our best!"

The twins bowed low.

Kasumi, Sally, and Maple all waved back.

And the twins turned to follow Iz.

"Whew… Okay, Maple. Seriously, how do you do it?"

"Yeah, how is that even possible?"

"I just used Atrocity and ran through the cave! Stomping all the monsters and trying to go as fast as I could!"

Maple's idea of best practices was beyond the average player's wildest imaginings.

Where others did things by the book, she took the book and threw it out the window.

"And, uh, how'd the fight go?" Sally asked.

Maple just looked puzzled.

"I mean, how'd they do with attacking, dodging, etcetera?" Sally clarified.

Maple thought about this, picturing their runs.

"Um...the dragon doesn't actually move much, so they didn't really do anything special. They did mention that they have trouble beating ordinary monsters. Dodging? Uh...they're about the same as me?"

That was the best Maple could manage.

But it was more or less what Sally had been expecting.

"Yeah, you can't really dodge with literally zero AGI. And they've got no shields... All right, my job'll be to get them some sort of evasion, but they're gonna be mostly attack focused."

Maple had gotten them the levels, so Sally was gonna focus on refining their technique.

"They can probably survive without dodging in this guild, but...can't hurt to learn a few tricks."

Maple Tree had the two best great shielders in the game.

And Maple had just picked up Martyr's Devotion, raising their defensive capabilities even further.

There were few forces as unfathomable as a durable Yui and Mai.

"Can't wait to see how they grow!"

"I'd better get ready to train them."

"I need to gain some levels myself... So much to do!"

"But that's what keeps it fun!"

"Good point!"

The more she had on her plate, the bigger Maple's smiles.

While they were talking, Yui and Mai had just reached the outside of Iz's workshop.

"In here," Iz said, opening the door for them.

Inside, it was quite roomy.

On one side was a desk Iz likely used when sketching new designs. On the walls were an array of weapons and armor, smithing tools, and the fruits of her labors.

In another corner was a set of flasks for making potions, wooden boxes filled with gems and crystals, planters growing all variety of things, and a sewing machine—clearly the tools required to craft anything this game allowed.

Iz found two extra chairs and sat down at her desk, turning to face the twins.

"Come in—have a seat. Let's decide what I'm making for you."

"Okay!"

"Please."

"Hmm, let's start simple—equipment stats."

"What do you think, Mai?"

"Good question… With the skills we have, do we keep boosting STR?"

Not long ago, they'd been considering abandoning the build concept entirely, but meeting Maple had allowed them to see a future down that path.

So they were at a crossroads.

How could they best support their guildmates? That would be the basis for this decision.

"When you're stuck and can't be sure what choice to make, just do what feels right. That's how Maple does it."

Iz had seen plenty of evidence that gut feelings could lead to dividends.

"Then..."

"Yes. Stay the course!"

Their minds made up, they spoke as one.

""Pure STR boost!""

Iz grinned, jotted that down, and it was time for the next step.

"Then let's decide what kind of equipment and what it should look like. I think you'll be using this gear for a while, so let's make sure we get it right."

As they talked things over, Iz rummaged through her boxes, showing them different pieces. They took their time settling on the right design.

Eventually she put down her pen, seemingly satisfied.

"Okay, we'll go with that. Wait right here. I'll craft them and be right back."

The gleam in her eye made it clear she couldn't wait to get cracking.

"Um, you're sure we don't have to pay?"

"You're good. But if it bugs you, I'll be happy to take any unwanted materials off your hands."

"We can do that!"

"We'll get lots!"

"Mm, good luck! There's plenty of good stuff on the second and third stratums. Well worth seeing for yourselves! Anyway, like I was saying, I'll have these done in a jiffy, so just wait outside."

""Okay!""

Once the two of them had left, Iz quickly went through her stock of materials, piling them up and getting ready to craft.

"The other guild members rarely stop by my workshop, so... good! I can go full tilt."

Iz set to work, never pausing, clearly having the time of her life. Maybe that's why their gear was finished far faster than she'd expected.

Outside the workshop, the twins had been waiting as instructed. Surprised by Iz's crafting speed, they happily received their new equipment. The outfits matched their hair—one set was black and green, the other white and pink. They were both quite cute, with several sets of frills and ribbon embellishments. Iz would be making them custom hammers, too, but currently she was out of materials, so those would come later.

Wondering what to do next, Yui and Mai headed back to the guild entrance but found no sign of the others.

"Where'd they go…?"

"Not sure… Whoa! We were talking for two whole hours!"

That was a lot longer than they'd thought.

"Should we call it a day?"

"Hmm… Mai, do you mind if we do one more thing?"

"…? Tour the second or third stratum?"

"No. I mean, we've got two new weapons. I wanna try them out!"

"Oh…right. Sure, let's do that."

"Thank you, Mai!"

They headed back to the first stratum to try out the very battles that had given them so much trouble before.

Back on familiar terrain once more, they began looking for a good place to fight.

"It's gotta be somewhere people won't see us."

"Mm…probably a good idea."

Outside of town, they quickly left the main path, heading toward the less popular mountains.

Avoiding areas where monsters might lay in ambush, they slowly traveled away from civilization.

"Careful, Yui."

"Got it, Mai."

Keeping their eyes peeled, each time they spotted monsters, they backed off before they were noticed. They did this again and again until they were certain there were no other players around.

They were in a zone of tall rock pillars near the base of the mountain.

They had not been aware this area existed, but it was perfect for what they were attempting.

"Nobody's here, right?"

"Not that I can see!"

Certain they were alone, they opened their inventories and hesitantly equipped the hammers Iz had given them.

"Wow. W-we truly can equip both…"

"It feels really weird having one in each hand."

Dual wielding their new hammers, they wove between the rocks, searching for monsters.

"…! Yui, there!"

Mai pointed—there was a two-yard-tall golem up ahead, basically a heap of rocks stuck together and imbued with life.

Monsters like this generally boasted high defense, but after coming all this way, it seemed worth the attempt.

"Okay. Let's do this, Mai!"

Yui's gaze was on it, too, and she was ready to go.

Mai nodded back—looking a bit nervous.

"Ready!"

"Okay!"

They dashed out from behind the rock, closing in on the golem.

It saw them coming and turned to face them, footsteps thudding.

""Supersize!""

Extra-large hammers swung at the golem, but the golem jumped back, causing the swings to sail through nothing but air.

And the golem was already charging back in, fist raised for a mighty attack.

"Yui!"

"I know!"

Not the most graceful attacks, but both of them brought their second hammer in for a sideswipe.

Their hammers pulverized the golem's bulky arms—and kept going, shattering the main body, too.

"Huh...?"

"Seriously?!"

With just a few blows, the golem turned to light—and vanished. It was far too easy. Both girls stood there flabbergasted.

"W-we really do a *lot* more damage..."

"Yeah. Even if we *did* land a hit, nothing's ever died that easily!"

Having two weapons equipped provided a serious offensive boost. And Maple had power leveled them—but Conqueror was definitely the biggest change.

That skill doubled their STR value. It was safe to say their DPS was at least three times what it had been before they joined Maple Tree.

"Wow! Just...wow. Augh!"

Yui had been jumping with delight but was too happy to notice the snake sneaking up behind her—until it bit her. Before she could even react, she had no HP.

There were a lot of monsters out in the field.

And with little experience, their ability to detect enemies was still rather poor.

"Yui!" Mai yelled, watching her sister disappear in a burst of light. She swung her hammers, but the snake easily darted around them and tackled her. She went flying.

She landed some distance away, skidding across the ground and raising a dust cloud.

"Ugh…"

The blow was more than her HP could handle, and she vanished in a puff of light just as Yui had. When she opened her eyes, she was back in the first-stratum town. She looked around and found Yui next to her—already down to a single hammer.

"Mai, you okay? Better put that away."

"Oh yeah. Right. Sorry."

Mai brought up her menu and put the extra hammer back in her inventory.

"The golem was slow enough for us to hit."

"Mm. But against something fast like a snake…we're still helpless."

They had plenty more challenges to overcome. They couldn't dodge at all, and their finesse with attacks left a lot to be desired.

"But if we *do* hit, we win. That's wild."

"I know, right? That's something!"

It might have been only one step forward, but that was progress nonetheless.

They could dominate any fight where their blows actually connected.

Previously, the only monsters they'd ever managed to hit were the bugs found just outside of town.

That golem had been way stronger. And from the looks of it, had a lot more defense. So one-shotting it had given them some much-needed confidence.

"And Iz said she'd make us some hammers that raise attack even more!"

"Right...great! That'll make fighting even easier!"

Hammers were definitely the way to go.

The road to true power had seemed impassible, but they felt certain that same road now lay open and waiting for them.

Like Maple earlier, they now had a ton of goals—and the busier you were, the more fun you had.

This was the most fun they'd had playing the game yet.

"Oh, right! Mai! We should sell the hydra drops and buy ourselves some skill scrolls."

"......!"

Mai's eyes went wide, and she nodded enthusiastically.

They'd never had money before, but that was no longer a problem.

"If we can attack with a skill..."

"That'll make our attacks even stronger!"

Eyes gleaming, they raced off toward the scroll shop.

They'd really never properly visited this store before—and now they had a whole wall of scrolls to choose from.

"First, let's sell this stuff."

"Yeah, I wonder how much we'll get?"

They sold half of what they had and came back to the scroll wall with five thousand gold.

"Um...we want attack skills, right?"

"Mm. I *think* so? But which one is strongest?"

They'd already made up their minds to learn the same skill, so that five thousand gold would have to cover two copies of the skill scroll.

"Well...how about this one?"

"Yeah, that looks good. We'll have to ask Sally and Maple about what else we should get."

They wound up picking an attack skill they could learn without breaking the bank.

"So Double Impact, then?"

"Let's go for it!"

Their minds made up, they each made a purchase.

Outside the shop, they quickly used the scrolls, learning Double Impact.

Double Impact

Two hammer strikes.
The resulting blows create small shock waves, dealing extra damage.

Usually, most players would be limited to just one hammer—but they could wield two. If they both used this skill together, it would unleash eight blows—each of which would one-shot the average monster.

And with their STR, those "small" shock waves would likely do considerable damage.

"Wanna try it out?"

"Yes! Right away!"

They headed back into the field.

When they reached a suitably deserted area, they tried their newly acquired skill.

The shock wave alone proved capable of taking down monsters, and the whole "as long as *something* hits" style was definitely working for them.

But after taking out a number of monsters, another surprise attack took them both down.

"Whew, still…that was fun! Wanna go again?"

"Sure! …Uh?"

They were about to head back out, but a thought made Mai pull up her menu.

And the color drained from her face.

"Er, uh…what's wrong, Mai?" Yui said, looking worried.

"Yui! W-we've gotta go! Or else…"

Mai's trembling finger was pointing at the time.

"Augh!"

Yui screwed up her eyes, wishing she hadn't seen that.

With all the time they'd spent in town and heading way out into the field, it was *very* late.

Way past the time they usually stopped playing. There was a strong chance their parents would be ready to give them a tongue-lashing the moment they left the game. Their post-log-out fate might be dire.

"We should probably hurry…and get it over with, right?"

"Y-yeah…"

They logged out and woke up in their own rooms.

The twins' rooms were across the hall from each other, and they opened their doors as one. They poked their heads out—and immediately found themselves face-to-face with their serenely smiling mother.

""Eep!""

"Good morning, girls. We need to talk. Come downstairs."

She turned her back and headed to the living room.

"It wasn't…"

"…all good."

Regretting their carelessness, they hung their heads and obediently followed their mother. Yui was racking her brain for a good excuse, while Mai had already given up.

◆□◆□◆□◆□◆

The day after the hydra grind, Yui and Mai were with Sally in the third-stratum Guild Home—this time, paying slightly more attention to the hour.

They were in a rather large room—specifically, the training room. This was a new Guild Home feature added with the implementation of the third stratum, and it was accessible only via a magic circle.

Here, your HP would never run out. You could use all your skills, but not learn new ones.

Since Iz had yet to craft hammers she deemed acceptable, the twins were still using the temporary ones. Both of them stood ready, a hammer in each hand.

"In this training room, you can practice fighting all you like without anyone seeing."

"Practice how?"

"You want to get better at wielding those hammers, right?"

""Yes...""

They were much stronger now, but the few fights they'd gotten stuck in (on the secluded outskirts of the first stratum) had taught them firsthand that their low AGI made avoiding attacks hard, and their fighting style was still less than ideal.

They had the strength to one-shot most monsters now, but their own HP was so low, they were in constant danger of being instantly knocked out by those same monsters.

"I'm gonna teach you how to dodge. And how to properly dual

wield. For the good of the guild, we at least need you to be capable of dodging piercing attacks."

As long as they could handle those, they'd be able to hold their own in any fight with Maple around.

"B-but we're not as fast as you, Sally."

This was the heart of the problem. Sally's AGI gave her a huge advantage.

On the other hand, Yui and Mai were both extremely slow.

"Yeah, if you don't know where the attack is coming from, neither of you will have any chance of dodging. But skills always follow a preset motion. Which means you can dodge those by a hairbreadth with a bit of training."

""W-we can?""

Both twins thought the same thing.

That was easier said than done, of course.

Otherwise, everyone in-game would be evading every skill attack.

"Well, I don't expect you to dodge everything. But piercing skills are another matter."

"Er...how so?"

"As far as I can tell, every piercing skill has a tiny lag between activation and execution."

Sally explained that most skills activated instantly after you said the name, but skills that did piercing damage had a slight but noticeable delay—something no other skills had.

Once they grasped the concept, Sally pulled two sheets of paper out of her inventory.

"These lists have the names of every piercing skill I'm aware of. Make sure you get those memorized before the month is out."

""W-will do!""

If they knew the skill names, they could take advantage of that brief lag and start dodging before the skill activated.

"But...that still won't be enough."

"I-it won't?" Mai asked, getting worried.

Sally had a bunch of wooden items in her inventory, and she took out one of these.

"I had Iz make us some spear-shaped poles. I'm gonna be swinging these around, so...it oughtta be good practice."

"Er...but I thought you could only use dagger skills?"

"Right. That's why I memorized the movements and speed for the ones I'll be using today. Then I just practiced until I could reproduce them."

""Uhhh...?""

That did not sound even remotely possible. An outlandish, impossible claim—that also happened to be entirely true.

"You both said you'd do whatever it takes to make yourselves useful, right? So we're gonna practice until you can dodge these. Ya dig?"

Yui and Mai's first tutor was Maple, and she'd left them with a legacy of the strange and unorthodox.

And now their second tutor, Sally, was trying to bequeath a portion of her flair for evasion.

Meanwhile, Maple was pacing around the guild interior.

"Kasumi! Have you seen Sally?"

"She's in the training room with the twins. You need her for something?"

Chrome and Kasumi were talking at the table.

"Hmm. I was thinking about checking around the third stratum with her, but...I guess I shouldn't interrupt."

Maple headed into town alone.

The others watched her go, then started whispering.

"I've got a sinking feeling she's gonna come back with yet another power-up."

"Do your hunches often come true?"

"Who knows…but you take your eyes off her for a minute, and she instantly gets stronger. Just like with Yui and Mai!"

"Fair. On that subject…have you seen Kanade lately?"

They'd both noticed he was spending very little time in the guild these days.

"Hmm… Supposedly, he's been hitting up the library on the second stratum. He went there a lot when we were based on that level, too."

Iz had said he often read books there.

"No telling where our members will wind up finding power-ups…," Kasumi said. She gave Chrome a meaningful look.

Or rather, his equipment.

He was another person who had a tendency to get stronger when people weren't looking.

She didn't say a word but was clearly a little jealous.

"Say a prayer to Maple, and you might get stronger, too," Chrome said. "I'm only half kidding."

"…I might seriously consider it."

While Chrome and Kasumi were talking, Kanade was in the very back room of a library many players had never once entered, flipping through the pages of a book.

The writing was not in Japanese—yet Kanade had just finished reading it, and he snapped the volume closed.

"Hmm," he said. "Very interesting."

He picked up the Rubik's Cube from the desk and gazed at it for a while, then put the book back on the shelf.

"So there are two more out there," he muttered.

He left the library, heading back into the wider second stratum.

Kanade arrived at the stratum's edge.

While he'd spent the bulk of his efforts on honing his support magic for the imminent guild-based battles, he'd also picked up several attacks spells to train so he could hold his own in a fight.

And Akashic Records could boost his offensive capabilities— though that very much depended on luck of the draw.

As a result, he had no trouble exploring solo.

"Plus, I drew good skills today."

Akashic Records had given him some particularly powerful magic.

He was busy excavating a stone dais, clearing away the sand so the surface was visible.

The information he'd found in the library had led him to this location.

"Hokay."

When he touched the dais, it vanished, revealing a staircase leading into the ground.

Kanade headed down it.

At the base of the narrow staircase, he found an old, decrepit door.

Behind that...was a library.

It was a lot like the library on the floating island—the one thing Kanade had cleared in the second event.

"Now, if I'm right, then back here should be... Yup, there it is."

Puzzle pieces scattered on an old table.

All white.

Kanade pulled them toward him, gathering them all into a pile.

There was a frame to put them in and letters written along the edge.

A divine trial.

Just like the floating island trial that had given him Akashic Records.

"Looks like…three thousand pieces. Way less than last time!"

He settled down on a chair, spread out the pieces, studying them… Then he began putting them together.

"Hmm, this goes here…and then that…and there."

White piece after white piece slotted into place.

It was like he already knew the answer.

After going at it for half an hour, he leaned back against his seat, pausing.

"Whew… This is exhausting. I might be getting a headache…"

Kanade was good at remembering things.

He had an excellent memory—perhaps too good.

Anyone else would have glanced at the pieces and thought they looked the same—but to Kanade, each one looked entirely different.

And he knew right away how the pieces were supposed to fit together.

The shapes of the connections and where each went.

Kanade remembered all of it.

But while recalling all that information was easy enough, actually retrieving those memories required extreme concentration.

And he could normally keep that up for maybe ten minutes at a time.

Under normal circumstances, he had a better memory than most—but this puzzle couldn't be solved without his absolute full focus.

He would just have to wait and rest.

"Can't take the books out of the library… If anyone else made it here, that would suck."

The lack of time compression was a big difference.

It would be a long while before he finished the puzzle, and he couldn't exactly spend the night here.

"I think I can get it done in time…but if I can't, I'll just have to come back tomorrow."

After a half hour of rest, Kanade started working the puzzle once more.

After alternating periods of intense focus and complete relaxation, he had the puzzle near completion.

Finally, the moment arrived… Kanade placed the last piece.

As he did, the white frame began to glow, and a Rubik's Cube rose up from within, twisting in the air.

"Oh-ho."

Kanade reached up, and it turned to streams of light, which flowed into his pocket.

"Ah… Since I have this already, they merged."

Kanade examined his equipment.

There was a new skill on his Rubik's Cube.

Sorcerer's Stacks

Allows magic or skills that require MP to be stashed as grimoires on a specialized bookshelf.

Any magic or skills stashed this way are unavailable until the grimoire itself is used.

Creating the grimoire requires twice the standard MP cost.

"Interesting… I'll have to try it when I get back. Wait…no, maybe not today. I'm awfully tired."

He went back up the stairs, pondering the books he'd read.

"The other one...wasn't on the second stratum. Maybe the third? Or the first...or not even implemented yet?"

Either way, Kanade was hell-bent on being the one who found it.

◆□◆□◆□◆□◆

The real-world admins were well aware that Kanade had learned this skill.

They were keeping close tabs on every member of Maple Tree, with a second set of markers reserved for anyone who'd done well in the first two events.

"Kanade cleared Our Bad Joke 20?!"

"Yeah...he did the same thing on the floating island."

"Why are we calling this a joke?! I designed it! It's a legitimate test of skill!"

"Maple Tree's apparently just stacked with people who can clear the toughest challenges one right after the other."

Chrome and Sally both had a unique series.

Kanade was taking on the libraries.

Even the newbie twins had grabbed STR-focused skills.

And Maple was everything.

Nearly all her skills were bad jokes.

"Uh...what else?"

"The first event top ten are...doing the same thing across the board. Maple especially. And a few who were close on their heels... But the new players are mostly acting the way we expected."

"Depending on the event, are we gonna need to partition off the top twenty?"

"That's a serious possibility at this point."

With that, he went back to staring glumly at his screen.

◆□◆□◆□◆□◆

Kanade had made up his mind to try out his new skill at a later date, but…curiosity got the better of him.

After emerging from the library, he headed away from the more populated areas.

"I happened to have Calamity Cannon today, so…Sorcerer's Stacks!"

Calamity Cannon

MP cost: 100.
High-powered frontal magic attack.
Ten-minute cooldown.

As Kanade evoked the skill name, light appeared in midair, coalescing into five cube-shaped bookcases.

The phantom sets of shelves floated around, phasing in and out of other objects.

A blue screen appeared in front of him, featuring a list of available MP-based skills.

"So for something like Fire Magic, which has several spells, I can choose on a per-spell basis, but for skills with no sub-skills, it's just the main skill name."

He went ahead and chose Calamity Cannon, at which point a thirty-minute timer appeared on his screen. Grimoire creation had begun.

Kanade used an item to recover his MP, then made a grimoire out of Fire Ball as well.

That would also take thirty minutes.

And each of these skills would be temporarily unusable in the meantime.

"So the half-hour creation time is a flat rate... Definitely something I'd have to pre-prep."

He spent half an hour reading a book.

When time was up, threads of light gathered above the screen, forming two books.

When he tapped them, they floated into place on the bookshelves.

"Hmm... Fire Ball!"

At his command, the red grimoire flew off the shelf, opened up, and shot a Fire Ball.

And the grimoire vanished.

"So you have to pay up front but can attack at no cost during combat. Now I'll just have to see if I can preserve this Akashic Records skill...and then find out if there's a limit to how many I can have stashed?"

Having investigated everything he wanted for the day, Kanade finally logged out.

The next day, he headed out to the field and checked Sorcerer's Stacks...and sure enough, there was still a single volume there. Proof he could keep an Akashic Records skill on hand.

Kanade was now capable of keeping any MP-based skill on file.

"Hmm. I'll have to regularly stock up, then. This oughtta let me throw out big spells nobody'll see coming."

With that in mind, he did his daily Akashic Records activation.

"I've always had good luck on the draw... Heh-heh-heh."

Half an hour later, he'd added a pitch-black grimoire to his shelves.

CHAPTER 7

Defense Build and Below the Cliff

Meanwhile, Maple was exploring the third stratum on her own.

Chrome and Kasumi were out hunting watermelons, while Yui and Mai were training with Sally.

Iz was crafting equipment, and Kanade hadn't shown his face around the Guild Home at all.

So Maple went out because she had nothing else to do.

The town was packed with machinery. Players were happily flitting about the skies in their flying machines. Looming in the center of town was a huge, imposing building—the town landmark. Maple looked around, wondering where to go first.

"Let's check out those machines!"

She headed for the NPC shop and looked at the machines everyone was using to fly.

There was quite a range. Car-like ones for whole parties, backpack-shaped ones for solo players. There were blue lights shining deep inside the machinery, suggesting the power source was some unknown technology.

Maple found one she thought was cool and went to buy it, but it was more expensive than she'd expected.

"Hngg... Awfully steep for a required item... It's a bit...no, that's a *lot* for me right now."

Maple didn't really grind for cash, so she was always in danger of going broke.

Her conclusion was inevitable.

"Yeah, let's not. I've got Syrup anyway!"

Maple could already fly without needing to rely on machines.

So for her, they weren't *actually* required.

Still, she was a curious girl, and she took her time examining all the new things this stratum had to offer.

And the more she looked, the more observations she made.

"These don't have any screws! How futuristic!"

Not only were they screwless, but they were all much lighter than she'd expected at first glance.

And if *Maple* thought they were light, they were *really* light.

After examining everything, she headed out.

Wandering the streets with no real goal in mind, she found an elderly NPC collapsed in an alley.

"Um...a-are you okay?"

Maple patted him on the back, and he began to whisper.

"Might I ask for some water? Could you spare a bit of food?"

When he asked like that, Maple wasn't about to refuse, so she took the requested items out of her inventory.

The old man took them, and she watched him eat and drink his fill.

"Whew...thank you. In return, might I offer you a story?"

"Huh? Uh, okay."

Maple settled down across from him, and he began his tale.

"You know that magnificent building at the heart of this town? There lies the Machine God. It creates all these flying contraptions."

"The Machine God? Tell me more!"

"Nobody understands how it makes these contraptions. There are those who have smashed them apart…but there was nothing inside that gave away the secret. No screws, gears, or springs."

"Wow! That's kinda creepy."

"Everyone in these parts knows that! But what they don't know is this…"

Intrigued, Maple hung on his every word.

"This is actually the *Second* Machine God."

"So there was a first…?"

"Yes. Once, this town was filled with ordinary machines. Before The First came, we knew nothing of machinery, but it brought us hope and dreams."

For a society with no reference for understanding technology, all machinery must have seemed like miracles.

"Then…one day, while I was away from town, I saw a pale light burst from the skies above the city."

"A-and…?!" Maple was leaning forward with anticipation.

"I hurried back, fearing the worst…and found the town flooded with new machines. No one remembered The First. And there was no sign of the old machines at all."

"So the light you saw robbed them of their memories? You were spared because you were too far away?"

"That concludes my tale. We are the only two who know The First existed."

"Well, thank you for sharing!" Maple said politely.

The old man shuffled off down the alley, vanishing into the maze of back roads.

"So did The Second hate The First? Doesn't seem like that triggered the start of a quest or anything, so… Maybe it'll be useful later?"

Maple filed the old man's story away in the back of her mind, then resumed exploring the town.

◆□◆□◆□◆□◆

The more Maple explored, the more she found machines made by the Second Machine God. Without exception, they had that same blue light gleaming within.

Otherwise, there wasn't much worth writing home about.

"Hmm...maybe it's time to check the field."

Outside of town, she found a highly vertical map, with sheer cliffs and mountain peaks obscured by clouds.

Very much impossible to explore without wings.

"Syrup! Let's head out!"

Maple opted for her usual approach.

The only difference was that she was no longer the only player flying.

"I guess if I just wanna take it easy and enjoy my flight, I can head back to the second stratum..."

Having all these other players buzzing around was definitely not the most relaxing thing in the world.

The most aggressive explorers had already found a dungeon, and most players were headed that way. They were all using flying machines, securely attached to their bodies.

Maple was just following the flow, unaware that the flow of traffic led to a dungeon.

"Where are we all going?"

Maple had no clue.

She didn't know why they were headed toward the mountains beyond these mist-shrouded cliffs...

Or about the sudden crosswinds.

"Waugh?! Uh-oh..."

With STR 0, Maple could hold on to Syrup's back for only so long.

The other players were all strapped into their machines—but Maple was just sitting astride her turtle. She had no defense against strong winds buffeting her.

So when the gust swept her off Syrup, all she could do was fall—headfirst.

"Aiiiiiieee! S-Syrup! Heeeelp!"

She couldn't see the ground. She wasn't even sure there *was* a ground.

Even Maple would take damage from a fall this high.

And despite her cries, Syrup wasn't fast enough to catch up with her.

"A-Atrocity!"

The only silver lining here was that the dense fog hid her outrageous skill.

In this form, no matter how much damage she took—it would just knock her back to her human body.

Far below, Maple was moving through the mist—still in monster form.

"H-huh? I didn't take *any* damage."

This was not a result of her notoriously high defense.

This area was clearly set to not cause any falling damage.

She switched back to her real body and pushed forward through mist so thick, she could barely see past an arm's length in front of her.

"Hmm? What's this?"

Her foot bumped into something, so she bent to pick it up.

It was a broken machine.

The remains of one anyway—all kinds of parts jumbled together.

Maple checked her map and found the name of the area.

"This is the…Graveyard of Dreams? I wonder if this is related to the old man's story?"

A hard-to-find hint.

And the hard-to-find item from the second stratum.

Both required conditions for reaching this location.

Conditions Maple had accidentally fulfilled.

"Welp… Best to proceed with caution!"

She threaded her way through piles of ruined machines, following the few walkable paths.

"The mist looks like it's thinning!"

Taking that as a sign, she went that way—and reached the depths.

She found herself surrounded by mountains of broken parts, with blue lights scurrying about—the same lights emitted by the machines in town.

And at the back of the area was an old man, leaning against a pile of destroyed machinery.

His body, too, was a machine, made up of countless gears, springs, and screws.

But he was too human to be a mere machine.

And yet, too machine to be considered human.

There was no light in his eyes, and half of one arm was missing—and there was a gaping hole in his chest.

"Yikes?!" Maple yelped.

The Bygone Dream—the mystery gear she'd found earlier—had suddenly left her inventory, moving unprompted.

It floated over to the man—and fit neatly into the hole in his chest.

Nothing else happened, so Maple gingerly approached.

"A-are you…with us?"

"Guh...gah..."

The instant Maple let her guard down, red light pulsed, and the man began to speak.

Maple flinched and hid behind her shield.

"I was king...the king of all machines... Crystallization of distant dreams and fantastical knowledge."

"............"

"I was king...in bygone days...before I was deposed."

Maple listened intently.

"I was... Wh-what was I...?"

But his speech was sputtering out. The red light faded. And then he lay still.

"D-did he break?"

Maple looked worried—and then a blue light fluttered down, enveloping the man.

It was absorbed into the hole in his chest...and then light gushed out.

"Guh...!"

There was a metallic screech, and the man began to move once more. Wreathed in a cold blue light, he quietly rose to his feet. The blue light grew stronger, and the red light faded.

"G-good, you're not broken!" Maple said happily.

But she soon sensed something amiss.

"I am...the king of the junk heap! I slumber amid the refuse... Dreams, miracles—are naught but garbage."

And then he transformed.

Scraps of junk flew in from all around, hurtling into the hole—and re-forming as weapons.

Loads of them. Every inch of him bristled with tools of violence—and every barrel pointed at Maple.

*   *   *

"Refuse…you will join the heaps!"

Maple realized the man in front of her was the First Machine God.

And he had clearly lost his mind.

"…Snap out of it!" she yelled, bracing her shield and drawing her sword.

She had a good idea what had made the god crazy.

That blue light—the one powering the Second Machine God's creations. The light that filled the town and now gleamed in The First's chest cavity.

"Gotta focus my attacks there!"

Maple made up her mind…

And her vision filled with pale-blue artillery fire.

◆□◆□◆□◆□◆

Maple's great shield did its job, and it briefly swallowed all the incoming fire, blowing right through her stock of Devour. Once it was gone, she wound up slammed against the wall.

"Whoa…that's some heavy knockback!"

These bluish bullets packed a wallop, and Maple didn't have the speed to avoid them. She quickly wound up pinned against the junk heap.

But they were unable to penetrate her defenses. So she was *only* stuck in place and not in immediate danger.

"Argh! I can't even move."

The bullets hammering against her were more of a pleasing

164

sensation than anything else, but the constant knockback was keeping her completely immobile.

"Hydra!"

Figuring it was worth a try, she fired a poison dragon at the Machine God, but...he was totally immune to the toxic effects. Hydra's impact itself did some damage, but there was no added damage from the poison.

"Ugh, now what?"

She was out of Devour and had used Atrocity when she fell.

Syrup was back in the ring, having fallen harmlessly after her the moment it was out of her skill's range.

But if she brought it out, it would just end up riddled with bullets.

Her remaining options were the ineffective Hydra, the Devour crystals, Predators, or Saturating Chaos.

Maple had incredible defenses and attacks that hit really hard, really fast—but she also had a clear and unavoidable weakness.

Specifically, she was not fuel efficient.

Maple's skill use was buffed by the zero-cost uses afforded by equipment skill slots, but those were finite.

She could not keep up her assault for long. And once she was out of skills, her offensive capabilities were drastically reduced.

Running out of skill uses was an ever-present problem that needed to be planned around, and she constantly ran the risk of finding herself in a situation where she wouldn't be able to defeat the monster—who in turn had no shot at defeating her. That would just make the battle one of pure attrition.

And unlike Hydra, she couldn't eat this foe.

Even Maple couldn't consume rusty metal.

That much was obvious.

"Martyr's Devotion!"

While piercing attacks were still a concern, Maple would have to rely on Predators and Syrup's attacks.

Since Hydra wasn't doing much good, she switched equipment sets.

With a tiara on her head and a white short sword in one hand, she drank a potion.

This put her HP at 650.

Her defense had dropped, but the bullets were still more friendly massage than deadly attack.

"Okay! Predators!"

Two monsters spawned, and Maple took a deep breath, focusing.

"Syrup! Giganticize! Mother Nature!"

At her call, Syrup made vines and mounds of earth grow from the ground.

These obstructions gave Maple a chance to find respite from the volleys of fire.

Then she charged toward the Machine God with what little speed she could muster.

Syrup's job was done, so she returned it to regular size.

But before she could reach her foe, another hail of bullets hit her.

"Whew!"

Hydra's ineffectiveness was not the only reason Maple had changed armor.

Martyr's Devotion came with a skill…

And a steep cost—600 HP.

"Aegis!"

A dome of light appeared around them, and for ten full seconds, any and all attacks were negated.

But as much ground as Mother Nature and Aegis combined let her cover, it still wasn't enough.

And the closer she got, the more intense the incoming fire—she would have to put a stop to that.

She had the Predators eat any weapons aimed at her, buying her some time.

New weapons were soon generated from nearby the scrap heaps, but that happened with a noticeable delay.

"Cover Move!"

While the weapons were being downed, Maple had sent Syrup (regular size) forward—and all she had to do now was warp to it.

She dismissed her Predators as she reached the Machine God's side in an instant; then she thrust her hand deep inside the blue-glowing chest cavity.

"This light is bad!"

Maple had her other arm around the Machine God, feeling inside it.

Her goal was to restore her opponent's senses while doing as little damage to him as she could.

"Saturating Chaos!"

A monster shot out of her palm, piercing her opponent's chest.

On the one hand, this was the right choice—on the other hand, it wasn't.

Attacking the chest wouldn't make the god less crazy. But it was the boss's weak point, so focusing attacks there did a ton of damage—and as a result, a change swept over the Machine God. Deep inside that chest cavity, beyond the remnants of the blue light—was a faint red glow.

This red glow grew stronger. And a voice echoed, machinelike but with a clear purpose behind the words.

"Gah...kahhh... I may be vanquished...yet..."

Maple listened intently, determined not to miss a single word.

"…While I still have a fragment of my mind restored…I bestow this upon thee, brave soul."

The blue glow was growing brighter once more.

"…Use my power…to defeat this vile creature…that once was me."

The Machine God turned toward Maple and tossed her old gear with a bright red gleam.

The same gear she had used to bring him back to life—

And this time, it was absorbed into Maple's body.

"…Let me…sleep…"

And with that, the Machine God changed again.

Pale-blue light covered his entire body. Where once he had been a wreck, he now turned to gleaming silver. His arms and back morphed like liquid, generating cannons and guns with no component parts. The blue light flared; then the form that clearly embodied the Second Machine God flew up into the sky, bristling with more weapons—and firing blue bullets down at her.

Like before, Maple was blasted back against the wall.

A mechanical voice grated above.

"Passing on power…is futile…"

Maple knew this must be The Second.

It had taken over The First's body and was forcing him to act.

"…Machine God…"

The skill the bygone deity had bestowed upon her. It was a simple power—nothing mysterious about it.

A change to Maple's equipment.

Playing things safe, she took off the tiara and Bonding Bridge, then switched back to her original short sword.

"Machine God!" she yelled. An image welled up inside her mind.

Maple chose her armor, great shield, and short sword.

The Second could make machinery from nothing, but The First required materials.

In other words…

The skill shattered her equipment and made weapons from it.

And of course, better components made more powerful equipment.

Maple whispered, "Full Deploy."

And black equipment materialized around her…

Innumerable weapons came into being, so black that they seemed hewn from the darkest night sky.

On the arm holding her great shield, gun barrel after gun barrel appeared in a series of thunderous clangs. On her back, a cannon aimed at the sky took shape, seemingly far too large for her to carry, like the bough of a venerable, ancient tree.

From the arm holding her short sword extended an equally black blade, and around her waist, an array of support armaments.

Gears great and small spun from her chest to her belly, and as the glistening panoply of weapons finished deploying, a fiery red aura sprang up around her.

"W-whoaaa… Wh-what is all this?!"

Maple gaped at her new equipment for a moment but then remembered the fight wasn't over.

"I have to beat that thing! Taunt!"

Maple put Bonding Bridge back on, called out Syrup, and had it generate vines and rock cover with Mother Nature, temporarily blocking The Second's attacks. At the same time, another set of vines grabbed Maple, carrying her toward her foe.

"Keep it up, Syrup!"

Pulling Maple along, the vines wove together, surrounding the two of them.

The Second soon found itself in a vine cage—which was closing in, forcing it and Maple together.

"Now you can't get away," she said.

Maple had inherited The First's power—she was The Third.

The newly born Machine God looked The Second dead in the eye and aimed all her weapons.

The Second readied all its weapons, too.

""Commence Assault.""

With a roar, flames spurted from every barrel and port. Blue and red lights strobed, filling the air with a dazzling fusillade.

These armaments might look like equipment, but they were not.

The power of them was determined by the sacrifice made—Maple's STR didn't factor into the output at all.

The strength of each shot was not that high—it was definitely quantity over quality.

At least, this time. She had multiple weapon types deployed—guns, cannons, and swords.

And it was obvious from the start which of them had endurance to spare.

As the vine cage burst, the blue lights and The Second machinery vanished from The First's form. As the Machine God went limp, Maple gathered him in her arms, protecting him as they drifted to the ground.

The First fell into a slumber, cradled in Maple's battery of machinery.

Maple quietly rose to her feet and leaned him and his constructs against the mountain of machines made from recognizable components.

"...You can rest now."

Certain the blue light was gone, she walked away, occasionally glancing back in The First's direction.

While Maple was slowly making her way back to the surface...

Four players were holding talks inside their Guild Home.

One had been the top-ranked player in the first event—Pain, a classic-looking knight in white armor with a silver sword. Many players called him the Holy Sword—a name derived both from his skills and his appearance.

Next was Dread, the man they called Godspeed. He'd taken second place in the first event—like Sally, he wielded daggers. His avatar boasted coppery-bronze skin.

Beside him was Frederica. She carried a wooden staff with a large jewel—making it clear she was a mage.

And the last member had ranked fifth in the first event.

Drag, the Ground Splitter. Rough armor and a massive, unadorned ax. His bulging muscles made it clear he was a powerful fighter.

The topic at hand—everyone in the top ten they had failed to recruit.

And the guild on everyone's minds—Maple Tree.

CHAPTER 8

Defense Build and the Crafter's Role

"Now, as for this…upcoming guild battle—there are two guilds we'll need to keep an eye on. First, the Flame Empire—in the first event, their members took fourth, seventh, eighth, and tenth. Second, while small, Maple Tree has the third-, sixth-, and ninth-place players from that event."

These two guilds contained most of the players capable of transforming a battlefield on their own.

"Maple Tree also has the blue girl who caused a stir in the second event, right?" Frederica asked. "She sounds like bad news, too."

Their spotty intel on Maple Tree left a lot to be desired.

They had next to no details on Sally and Kanade.

"Depends on the specifics of the event format, but we could just crush 'em with numbers. Worse comes to worst, we send you in, Pain."

Dread had a point. Maple Tree was quite small, but *their* guild was massive in comparison.

Numbers alone meant they'd always have the advantage.

"Our guild has solid strength across the board," Drag said. "And we've had 'em all get Poison Resist; those who had the time picked up Paralyze Resist, too. That means Flame Empire is the real threat."

"And we've got our crafters running that dungeon and making gear for everyone, right?" Frederica was talking about the second dungeon found on the third stratum. Only crafting classes could enter, and the materials found within allowed—for the first time—crafting of gear with skills attached.

They had parties running through the place around the clock, churning out gear with status-effect-resisting skills.

"This Maple girl's all about status effects and her shield, right? Plus that turtle? They say she's a full VIT build, which sounds crazy, but...odds are we can shut her down completely."

"Hmm... Well, Frederica, any information you can gather will help. Especially on Maple Tree."

"You worry too much, Pain! I got this."

Frederica picked up her staff and left the room.

Dread and Drag followed.

Left on his own, Pain muttered, "There's nothing more frightening than what you don't know. We know too little about Maple Tree."

He did not know about Chrome's new gear.

Or Kanade's magic.

He'd yet to face Sally's evasion.

They didn't even know Yui and Mai existed, let alone the level of destruction they were becoming capable of.

And worst of all...

Nearly all members were convinced Maple could attack only with poison and her shield.

They did not know about her angel form, monster form, Machine God form, or Syrup's laser death beams.

Pain alone had a hunch there was more to her—but he lacked evidence to back that up.

◆□◆□◆□◆□◆

While Pain was fretting over Maple Tree, Iz was fidgeting on a chair in their Guild Home, her waist-length blue hair swaying.

She had just heard the breaking news about the crafter dungeon.

While she spent most of her time indoors, this lead was very tempting.

"Urgh... If I could get Maple or Sally to help..."

She meant borrowing Syrup and Oboro.

With the two of them, there was little risk of dying mid-dungeon.

Dying meant a loss of gold, some items—and worst of all, a temporary stat drain.

She would rather avoid that.

But of course, neither girl was anywhere to be seen.

Iz managed to wait all of five minutes.

Hitting the limits of her patience in no time at all, she stuffed her inventory full of combat equipment and gathering items, then flew the coop.

A five-minute machine-wing flight later...

She was in the new dungeon.

"Okay...let's do some mining."

Iz quickly found ores and crystals to hammer away at.

Crafters were unable to learn any weapon skills or magic, but a whole range of skills exclusive to their class made up for that restriction.

These included Smithing and Synthesizing.

However, these could be used only in workshops.

Synthesizing was an exception; anything craft-able below level V could be made anywhere, but the necessary ingredients still had to be assembled, and some items had carry limits.

For instance, bombs were an invaluable offensive tool for any crafter, but they could be made only in a workshop, and each player could carry only five.

Even with healing potions, crafting in the field was limited to the two weakest kinds.

And if that wasn't bad enough, there was a permanent reduction to all weapon damage.

To make up for it, crafters got experience each time they completed anything made with skills like Smithing.

But they were undeniably lousy at fighting.

Crafters were, by and large, people who didn't mind that. They just focused on making items instead.

Iz was no exception.

And she was a top-tier crafter.

Since the day the game launched, she'd been mining, smithing, sewing, gathering, and synthesizing, raising every crafting skill available, sometimes getting so engrossed, she played all night long.

Time turned to strength, and it wasn't long before no one could match her in sheer crafting prowess.

But the flip side of that was that she'd barely leveled Throw— one of the few attack skills crafters had.

Throw was a skill that amplified damage done by literally throwing knives or other items.

Iz had focused so heavily on gathering items that her Throw skill had remained worryingly low.

"Ooh, there's a fishing spot over here."

Iz took out her rod and started fishing.

She was catching fish that dropped materials she'd never seen.

Her eyes lit up like an excited child's.

Iz had made this rod herself.

This dungeon's materials allowed players to craft equipment with skills attached, but that was very specifically equipment.

It had already been possible to attach skills to other certain items.

For example, Iz was carrying a pickax and fishing rod that both had a boost to rare item drops, a very high endurance, an increase in the overall drop quantity, and a boost to gathering speed—an impressive lineup, to say the least.

She'd spent a great deal of time and materials crafting it, and items like that had helped keep her ahead of her competition.

When she was done fishing, Iz headed farther in.

"No monsters around, huh? Lucky for me, but…"

It made sense that a crafter-only dungeon wouldn't be filled with foes no crafter could beat.

As a result, monsters spawned only in specific sections of the dungeon.

It was entirely possible to avoid fighting anything but the boss.

In one room, she encountered a monster with crystals on its back but avoided engaging.

Iz already had intel on the dungeon boss.

She knew that when she entered the boss room, a magic circle would already be there—allowing you escape without defeating the boss. And she knew that the crystals covering the boss were great materials, and you could harvest them with a pickax.

She could probably take out the other dungeon monsters with

that same pickax, but she didn't want to lower the durability without good reason.

Avoiding all monsters and gathering whatever she could, Iz reached the boss room door and pushed it open.

The room was covered in beautiful, glittering white crystals.

And in the back was a huge lizard, uncurling—its back covered in crystals of the same hue.

"I'm gonna help myself to those. Sound good?"

Iz hefted her pickax menacingly.

"Ho...kaaay!"

Iz easily avoided the lizard's charge, swung her pickax, and leaped away again.

Maple was basically the only player completely ignoring the concept of dodging; even crafters like Iz were making judicious point investments into AGI.

And this lizard was slow enough for her to easily evade its attacks.

When she turned back toward it, she noted the dent she'd made in its HP.

"Good intel, then. And I think my pickax should be durable enough!"

Her pickax was a masterpiece born from time and luck.

And by her calculations, she should be able to smash all the lizard's crystals with it.

Unfortunately...the fewer crystals it had, the faster the lizard got.

Whether it would get too fast for her to handle...

"If I could dodge like Sally does, it would be so easy!"

Dodge a charge, whack a crystal, rinse and repeat.

After a while, the lizard's movement pattern changed. It started running across walls or climbing onto the ceiling and trying to drop on her, crystals first.

"Oh, got yourself stuck? Perfect!"

The ceiling drop left the jagged crystals embedded in the floor, and it took the lizard a minute to free itself.

And that gave her ample time to swing her pickax.

She even tossed a bomb on its exposed belly—unfortunately, this didn't deal any damage.

"Shame. Just because it looks soft doesn't mean it's actually a weak point."

The info has said attacks were ineffective, but she hadn't been sure how far they'd experimented. The faster she could wrap up the battle, the better—but not every long shot paid off.

Iz went back to mining.

A cheaper pickax would have fallen apart by now, but Iz's still had three-quarters of its durability remaining.

She was now keeping her distance, mining only when it was stuck in the ground.

Just standard evasion tactics.

Sally's thing where she dodged at the last second and landed a counter was, frankly, freaky.

"Would be nice if I could make Maple some gear with autoheal on it... Hmph!"

There was a crack, and another crystal shattered, adding itself to Iz's stash.

She kept at this, the lizard getting steadily faster—until she was unable to dodge in time and got knocked aside.

"Oof. Can't tank a second one of those..."

Iz's accessory slots were entirely filled with Item Pouches.

An Item Pouch could hold specific types of items for two hours, and Iz had stuffed all the pouches with potions.

But as the name implied, they didn't have an amazing capacity—only five items per pouch.

Still, they sped up the recovery process, which was huge.

"Whew… Gonna have to use Quick Fix once…no, twice."

She was carefully comparing her pickax durability and the lizard's HP.

Quick Fix was a skill that restored item durability—but not by a lot.

But Iz's pickax was much more durable than your average one, so using Quick Fix on it was the equivalent of a major repair to a normal pickax.

"I'll have to do it while it's stuck."

Each time she took damage, she chugged the best potion she had on hand.

And swung her pickax every opening she got.

A few minutes later, it did the ceiling drop again.

"Quick Fix."

With the pickax's durability topped up, Iz attacked…

And the next time it got stuck, she looped through the same motions. Certain she could hold out, she focused on attacking, chipping away at the lizard's HP.

Her math proved accurate.

The lizard's HP was now low enough that a visual comparison of its health bar and her pickax's durability made it clear which would give out first.

"Just a few more hits… Don't blow it, now."

Iz focused on not dying.

No use being stingy with potions—and no use worrying about a few injuries here and there.

And at long last, the lizard went down.

"*Haah...haah...!* Never soloed a boss before... I'm never gonna be a fighter. I made the *right* choice focusing on crafting..."

Her pickax was about to break, but she'd done the math right—so not a problem.

"Whew... Well, I've definitely got enough for our guild. Time to go... Oh?"

When she turned toward the magic circle, she found a treasure chest waiting.

She approached with caution, knelt down, and tapped the surface.

"The intel didn't mention any chests...but I guess I'll just have to open it!"

She popped the lid and found an antique-looking long coat, a big pair of goggles, and a set of boots inside.

Iz put them in her inventory and read the descriptions.

"Ohhh...so that's why none of them ever ask for repairs."

Alchemist Goggles

[DEX +30] [Indestructible]
Skill: Faustian Alchemy

Alchemist Long Coat

[DEX +20] [AGI +20] [Indestructible]
Skill: Magic Workshop

Alchemist Boots

[DEX +10] [AGI +15] [Indestructible]
Skill: New Frontier

Faustian Alchemy

Allows the exchange of gold for select materials.

Magic Workshop

Allows workshop use in any location.

New Frontier

Allows the creation of new items.

Iz immediately equipped the new gear and took the magic circle to the exit.

Someone in her position could rake in gold hand over fist, and she could use that to generate gunpowder or herbs at will.

And she could now use high-level crafting anywhere.

That meant she could craft and Throw as many bombs as she liked, allowing her to fight like no other crafter in the game.

While Iz was pickaxing the lizard, Maple arrived back at the Guild Home.

"Hmm... Well, I'm back...but there's nothing to do here. Guess I'll go for a walk?"

While she was plotting her next move, Sally came in the door behind her, and Yui and Mai emerged from in back.

"Oh! Would the three of you like to join me for a nice midair stroll?"

"A wha—? No, you know what? Sure, why not?"

""We'd love to!""

They all readily agreed, so the four girls headed out together.

Yui and Mai elected to ride on Syrup's back, so Sally joined them. The twins liked Syrup better than the machines.

Sally idly mused that anyone who'd do an extreme build probably thought alike.

"Everyone on board? Then here we go!"

Maple made Syrup levitate, and they flew off.

"What have you been up to, Maple?"

"Oh...I met a god."

""What...?!""

They had been expecting something *slightly* more earthbound.

Sally was the first to reconnect her jaw.

"So...what'd you pick up this time?"

She figured it would be best to be in the know.

"Well, if I go full-bore, it'll be a bit much, so...just a peek! Deploy Left Arm!"

Destroying her gear could give her much more powerful weaponry a set number of times.

A whole slew of guns appeared around her left arm.

"Whoa... Holy crap..."

"I can shoot them! I won't, though."

"Th-that's really something..."

Maple dismissed the armaments before any other players saw.

"Save that for the guild fight."

"You betcha! I'll make up for that third event! You're both in, right?" Maple smiled at the twins.

""W-we are!""

"Yeah, they'll be sticking to you like glue. Gotta keep that Martyr's Devotion on 'em."

"Yes! We're practicing dual wielding, too!"

They both looked delighted. They'd escaped the doldrums of being completely helpless and were now literally doling out instant death to their enemies as long as their blows connected.

And with two hammers each, all they had to do was wave them around in a general direction and watch as monsters went down like dominoes.

Post-leveling, they could play without dying nearly as much, and they were having a lot more fun.

"Hmm, Maple, there's a lake below."

"Oh? Wanna check it out?"

The twins nodded, so Maple set them down by the shore.

They all bent over, dipping their hands in the water. Yui and Mai set their insane hammers on the ground and sprawled out next to them. This sight made a very different impression whether the focus was the girls or their weapons. The soft lapping of the water would have been just as refreshing in the real world.

"What'll this event be like?"

"If they're doing the time-compression thing, it'll definitely be longer than a day... Huh."

Sally trailed off, then slowly rose to her feet.

"What's up?"

"Is there something coming?"

"Yeah—just a player. Following us."

Sally peered around the edge of a nearby boulder.

And found a player with a blond side ponytail. Frederica.

"Whoops…you caught me."

"Why are you following us?" Maple asked, puzzled.

The twins looked equally baffled.

"Probably recon for the guild battle," Sally said. "Our guild has so few members, we don't leak easily."

The more people you had, the harder it was to keep secrets. Big guilds tended to leak all over.

"Well, since you followed us, I've got a proposition."

"Oh? What?"

Sally leaned in, whispering conspiratorially.

"Care to give us some info on The Order of the Holy Sword? Or Flame Empire?"

The former was Pain's guild—in other words, the same one Frederica was in.

Frederica started warily backing away.

"Wh-why would I wanna do that?"

"Hook me up, and I'll be willing to Duel you. You need intel on me, right? Tease it out of me in combat or…if you win, I'll answer any single question."

Frederica had to think about that one.

A Duel was a PVP fight with formal, binding rules.

Moreover, Sally had a point—they didn't have much concrete info on her.

Fighting someone was a good way to glean a lot of firsthand information about them, so this was too good an opportunity to pass up.

And if she leaked info on Flame Empire to them, that made it more likely Maple Tree and Flame Empire would thin each other out.

She could weaken both their major foes at once.

And all for the price of a little information.

Even if Sally refused the Duel and ran off, Frederica still came out ahead.

"Okay, you're on. I've only got info on Flame Empire, but here goes…"

Frederica told Sally everything she had on the other guild. No embellishments or distortions.

That would make it easier for Maple Tree to hurt them.

And some of that info was especially valuable.

"Really, a trapper? First I've heard of that class."

"Ready to keep your end of the bargain?" Frederica said, figuring Sally would back out.

Clearly, it was in her best interests to take the info and run.

"Okay, offer's up."

"Huh? O-oh, right."

Blinking, Frederica accepted the Duel.

The rules transported the two of them to a battle zone. A simple death match—they'd fight till one of them ran out of HP.

Magic circles appeared before them, and both girls vanished.

Maple and the twins were left behind gaping.

"Wh-where'd they go?"

"Maple! I think this is a Duel! I read you can have fights like that!"

"Y-you can?!"

Yui explained that they'd be back once the fight ended, so the three of them settled down to fish awhile as they waited.

Of course, all three had extreme builds and were terrible at fishing.

Meanwhile, the duelists found themselves in an arena.

On their arrival, Frederica said, "If I win, you'll answer any one question?"

"Of course. Cross my heart!"

Frederica looked her dead in the eye. She didn't detect any hint of a lie.

Still unsure what Sally's goal was, she decided to feel out Sally's abilities while hiding her own.

And if she saw a chance to win, she'd take it.

"On ten?"

"Sounds good."

Ten seconds later, their Duel began.

One minute into the fight...

Frederica was chain casting, watching Sally closely all the while.

"Hmm... She's definitely hard to hit."

In fact, Frederica had yet to land a single spell.

But it didn't seem like she *never* would.

Sally was performing big, flashy dodges, but these were risky moves, and it didn't look like she could parlay those maneuvers into attacks.

"...I'll give her another minute, then take her out."

Frederica did just that and was suitably impressed by Sally's evasive capabilities.

She'd thrown some skills into the mix between a few spells but once again failed to land a single hit.

But this was hardly Frederica's full power.

"Multi-Firebolt!"

At her cry, an array of magic circles appeared around her, each shooting missiles made of fire.

Frederica had assumed this would be more than enough to finish Sally off.

"Attack Lure!" Sally said, just loud enough for Frederica to hear it.

And no sooner had the words left her mouth than her movements changed completely. It was enough to make her think the firebolts were the ones avoiding Sally.

Like something was protecting her, leading them astray—every bullet missed by a fraction of an inch.

The riskiness of her earlier moves vanished, and before Frederica knew it, those daggers were swinging right at her.

"Multi-Barrier!"

Dozens of gold magic circles appeared right in front of the mage, barring the daggers.

One barrier went down, then another—Sally made it through *five*.

Then she jumped back, wary of possible counters.

"Didn't plan on using that, but...I guess I can live with revealing Multi-Barrier."

Frederica was definitely *strong*.

Strength gave her confidence.

And her experience told her Sally's Attack Lure must be a skill.

And a good one—but the best skills always had a long cooldown.

Those daggers were awfully strong, too. Another valuable piece of intel.

But Frederica was unaware...

That the Attack Lure skill did not exist.

Sally had faked it.

She'd actually simply observed the attacks and avoided them naturally.

Nothing more.

"Multi-Waterbolt!"

Frederica's next spell summoned water projectiles.

Sally was forced to run, even resorting to Superspeed to dodge the volley just in the nick of time.

Frederica even saw her go into a roll to avoid the last few.

And she took that as proof that Attack Lure's cooldown was several minutes long.

Sally's deception was worming its way deep into the mage's mind.

"Multi-Stonebolt!"

Frederica's thoughts had already turned to what she should ask once she won.

Sally was out of breath. She lost her balance—there was no way she could avoid the stone bullets now.

"Got her!" Frederica breathed a sigh of relief...

And she heard Sally yell, "Waterflow!"

Before the mage's eyes, Sally started batting all the rocks aside with her daggers.

A different approach from the waterbolts...suggesting that this skill worked only on solid objects.

This interpretation...was also meaningless.

As Sally batted the last stonebolt aside, she shot forward only to have her attack cut short.

"Right. I'm gonna surrender."

"What? Oh. Okay..."

The words You Win! suddenly appeared in front of Sally—and they were just as quickly sent back to where they'd started.

"Bye!" Frederica said. She waved and walked away.

A safe distance from her opponent, she started muttering under her breath.

"Ugh, she forced me to use Multi-Barrier! If I kept fighting, I was bound to let more slip... Yeah, best to quit while I was ahead."

Frederica remained convinced she'd learned a lot about Sally.

At the least, she believed she'd learned far more than she revealed.

She never realized which of them was caught in the bigger mousetrap.

Sally watched Frederica go, whispering, "The better you are, the easier it is to fake a disadvantage. Heh-heh-heh."

She's seen the mage twitch when she said "The Order of the Holy Sword" and immediately suspected where her loyalties lay.

And when Frederica had started blabbing info on the Flame Empire, Sally took that as proof she was with The Order.

What the mage did would work to her guild's advantage.

Playing other guilds against each other was also in Sally's play-book, so it wasn't hard to figure out Frederica's plan.

"And 'knowing' false info is worse than knowing nothing."

Sally now knew about Frederica's offensive spells, her impressive MP pool, and her significant defensive abilities.

And Frederica had learned about Attack Lure and Waterflow—two fearsome skills with exploitable weaknesses.

Or rather—Sally had successfully planted the seed of false intelligence about these nonexistent skills.

The mage was so confident in her own strength that the sight of Sally's desperate evasion rolls had pulled the wool over her eyes—and she'd left without learning a single real thing.

Frederica was *good*—but Sally was far better.

"Pride blinds us all… Gotta look out!"

Sally turned and headed over to her friends.

"I'm back."

"Oh, there you are! All done?"

"Yup. Pulled off what I wanted, then sent her packing. Think I'll fish with you guys for a bit."

She joined them at the water's edge.

Sally's rod alone was pulling in fish like crazy.

"You know, Maple, you haven't seen Yui and Mai fight since they got stronger. Oh, got a bite!"

"No, but I hear you've been getting them good and ready."

In Sally's opinion, if the twins got a little more experience with dual wielding, they'd be perfect.

Right now, their abilities were like a weaksauce blend of Maple's and Sally's hellfire, and in extremely specific situations, they could unleash a downright unreasonable level of force.

"Wanna see them in combat? We could find a place without prying eyes."

""Let us show off!""

"Then maybe the forest? Not many people there. Especially if we head away from dungeons."

"Sounds like a plan."

The four of them hopped on Syrup's back and wafted off to the deserted forest depths.

"Here we are!"

They landed in a forest clearing.

It was big enough for the twins to swing their hammers freely. They each took out their second hammers and stood ready.

"We'll be keeping our distance."

"Good idea."

Monsters were already approaching through the underbrush.

Yui and Mai started swinging—not even using any skills.

Any successful strike spelled instant death, and the hammer blows were raining down mercilessly on any and all monsters.

A monster darted sideways, avoiding Yui's blow, but Mai spotted it instantly, and her follow-up made it explode.

If Mai left an opening, Yui covered it. The hammers had impressive range, and the girls took full advantage of that. Sally had shown them a few tricks, and they thought alike to begin with—so their teamwork was now genuinely impressive.

And there were no monsters around that could tank one of their blows and keep coming.

All they had to do was hit once. That took a lot of the stress out of fighting.

Slaughtering all before anything could get to them.

"Those attacks are so good!"

"This is what everyone thinks when they see your defense, Maple."

"Oh...huh."

Even as they spoke, more monsters joined the carnage.

And when the dust finally settled, they hopped back on Syrup and flew away.

In the air, all four got a message—simultaneously.

It was from the admins, detailing the next event.

They read through it.

"Time compression—once again, no way to join in late."

"Five days this time, huh? A bit shorter."

And then the meat of the message...

At last they learned what this guild event would actually involve.

First, guild sizes: Less than twenty members were classified as "small." Twenty-one to fifty as "midsize." And fifty-one or more as "large."

*   *   *

Each guild was given an orb to defend, and other guilds would attempt to steal these.

When defending your guild's orb, each six-hour stretch earned one point.

Small guilds would earn two points.

When in possession of another guild's orb, each three-hour stretch earned two points. And the guild robbed of their orb would lose one point.

If the orb was stolen by a small guild, the orbless guild would lose three points.

If the orb was stolen by a midsize guild, the orbless guild would lose two points.

Once points were awarded, the stolen orb would automatically return to its original location.

If the orb was recovered within the three-hour limit, no points were awarded or lost.

It was possible to check the locations (and status) of guild members and your guild's orb on the map screen.

Stolen orbs were automatically placed in the pilferer's item list.

Smaller guilds would be positioned in easy-to-defend locations.

Several temporary guilds had been created, and players not in guilds could apply to these, allowing them to join the event.

Next, the death penalty.
First death: 5 percent stat reduction.
Second: another 10 percent drop.
Third: another 15 percent penalty.
Fourth: 20 percent on top of that.
Fifth: retired!

If all players were eliminated, the guild's orb would no longer spawn.

You could steal the same guild's orb only once a day.

That was the gist of the rules.

"Hmm, so five deaths and you're done, and frankly, starting from three onward, you're pretty hosed. At four deaths, your stats are halved..."

Given Maple Tree's numbers, they couldn't afford to use any strategies that involved sacrificing themselves.

Large guilds might have little to fear from death, but they didn't have that luxury.

"That means we'll want to leave some of us on defense, but... this is gonna be rough. Still, if we're smart about our offensive moves..."

"What's so rough about it?"

"First, we don't have enough people to mount an offense. Or man the fort. Also—and this is the biggest problem—we're all gonna get real tired. We'll be facing constant attacks. Even at night. Without numbers, it'll be hard to even get any shut-eye."

They'd be badly nerfed every time Maple took a nap.

But as long as Maple was around, they could pin their hopes on defending stolen orbs.

"I see... Last time they compressed time, there weren't too many people who focused on attacking other players, but this time, it'll be constant fighting."

And the longer players were stuck in combat, the more mistakes they'd make. In Sally's case, that directly impacted her evasion capabilities—and that could be dire.

And there was bad news for Maple, too.

"Before the event is up, they'll have figured out about the Devour nerf. Once you run out of skill uses...if they realize *most* of your skills are limited, then we could be in trouble."

If Maple was on the front lines all day, she'd definitely run out of big skills.

Peak danger would visit them at the end of each day.

"Right..."

"How long we can keep your deal a secret might be the key to the whole event."

Many of Maple's skills could serve as the ace up their sleeve—especially since nobody knew about them yet.

Their strategies would have to revolve around keeping these under wraps as long as possible. Delaying tactics, running where necessary—whatever it took.

"Maple, Yui, and Mai—you'll all be on defense. None of you are exactly covering a lot of ground in the field...and we could probably stick Kanade with you, too."

"We'll have to discuss the details once we're back home."

The twins nodded.

Since neither of them had done a time-compression event, Sally and Maple filled them in on the concept as they headed back.

The news of the new event sure gave them a lot to talk about.

And of course, Maple Tree's members were not the only ones talking. Every guild was trading information about the top players. The three guilds studded with the stars of the first event dominated the chatter.

The Order of the Holy Sword. Flame Empire. Maple Tree. Everyone was worried about those three guild masters.

"Flame Empire's guild master—Mii. Her DPS is insane. She doesn't even count as a mage anymore!"

"When Misery is with her, she never runs out of MP. Gotta split 'em up somehow..."

"And The Order has tons of high-level players, so they can dominate with numbers alone. Just gotta avoid coming in contact with 'em."

"Then there's Maple... She's, uh...in a league of her own, you know?"

"Yeah. At the very least, we gotta get Poison Resist... I'm hearing her big attacks are limited. If you can't beat her, you can always run away. She's *slow*."

Everyone nodded. No need to face Maple head-on. Coax out her biggest attacks and run if you were in trouble. Let sleeping dogs lie.

"...What if she's on the offensive?"

"That's like asking what if the Demon Lord shows up in the starting village."

"...Fair."

Those talking had no idea that the Demon Lord from their hilarious metaphor had assembled a council of formidable minions whose powers compensated for her weaknesses.

Maple might be in another league, but she was far from alone.

◆□◆□◆□◆□◆

Unaware they were already a huge topic of conversation throughout the server, Maple Tree wrapped up their own event-planning session and single-mindedly threw themselves into the necessary preparations.

Fortunately, all members were able to play that day, so they'd divvied up roles accordingly.

Maple, Yui, Mai, and Iz would be guarding their base.

Sally, Chrome, and Kasumi were on the offense.

And Kanade was a switch-hitter.

Chrome and Kasumi were out hunting monsters, gathering drops.

This was both keeping their senses honed and helping ensure Iz had a solid reserve of cash on hand.

Sally had left the Guild Home, saying she was off to do some evasion training.

Yui and Mai were in a deserted corner of the second stratum, practicing their coordination.

Iz had asked Kanade to gather ingredients for top-tier MP potions, so he'd headed out into the field in search of those.

Everyone had told Maple to explore as she saw fit, so she was aimlessly wandering the third stratum, gathering drops as she went.

Sally was alone in a high-encounter area of the second stratum.

All she was doing was dodging attack after attack. The blue aura around her was at full strength, never once fading.

Trying to extend the length of time she could stay focused, she was moving with unerring precision.

Fortunately, she was still in school, and this was summer vacation, so she could play as long as she liked.

"............Whew!"

She claimed the life of a monster with a strike so powerful, it was hard to believe it came from a dagger. A new foe swiftly took its place.

Sally kept moving. Trying to reach her self-imposed goal.

"...Mm, let's see if I can go all night."

Certain this was the right choice, she kept on pushing herself.

Yui and Mai were also fighting on the second stratum.

Their plan required keeping Maple in reserve, and they'd play a key part in ensuring that was possible. They were super fired up about how crucial their performance was to the whole plan.

Iz had finished the hammers to go with their new gear—each of them now had two massive hammers that matched the color of their hair and were decked out in pure-white and pitch-black gear, respectively. This equipment looked like adorable clothing—the white set had pink ribbons, and the black had green. A pleasing mismatch with the dual hammers of destruction.

In their accessory slots were two rings and a ribbon.

Each of these was raising STR, making their build even more attack-centered.

Right now, they were focused on protecting one another, but with Maple supporting them, they could abandon all defense and unleash a brutal amount of force.

Unaware of their stats, there would likely be players who tried to block their attacks with shields.

Depending on the shield's qualities, that might well make the shield explode.

That ought to induce panic in any opponent.

Although they'd likely be dead before they figured out what hit them.

"Double Impact!"

The pounding refrain of their skill was total overkill.

They'd also learned several new skills recently.

One of these…was Throw.

Their inventories were filled with basketball-size iron balls, courtesy of Iz.

But those were for a later occasion.

Told to entertain herself, Maple was busy leveling Syrup and having Hydra destroy her equipment.

Once it had all been destroyed, she'd be able to activate Machine God again.

And that would raise her defense.

This had become her daily routine in the run-up to the event.

"Oh! Syrup, you leveled up!"

She gave it a pat on the head and a smile.

"Another new skill! Rampart?"

This skill generated indestructible walls around whoever had Bonding Bridge equipped. These would last thirty seconds.

Maple tried it out. Instantly, towering walls appeared all around Maple—about two yards from her.

Didn't seem like she could attack easily with those up, but neither could her foes.

From the enemy's perspective, it was like an egg—

And whatever hatched from it was bad news.

"I wonder what skills Oboro's learning… How awesome is it now?!"

Once Maple had Hydra smash her equipment, she went off to buy a skill scroll she'd been eyeing for a while.

The skill in question: Pierce Guard.

This was a countermeasure against piercing attacks that hit her great shield.

This skill allowed her to null the piercing damage.

She'd been too busy to pick it up before, but she hadn't forgotten about it.

They were done strengthening the guild itself, and Kanade had been stocking up on grimoires.

Iz had a satisfactory heap of gold and had crafted a solid number of the items New Frontier provided.

Sally had pushed through her exhaustion and completed final adjustments.

Chrome and Kasumi had gathered all the watermelons they needed to raise the guild STR, AGI, and INT boosts to the current max.

Maple had become tankier than ever, while Yui and Mai had learned how to hit even harder.

Just as everyone had done everything they could to prepare, the day of the event finally arrived.

All eight of them would be participating.

"Let's try and win this thing!"

"You got it!"

This was their first team event since they'd founded the guild.

They were ready to prove what a small team of elites could accomplish.

Light surrounded the eight of them…and they were swept off to the battlefield.

AFTERWORD

Let me start by thanking anyone who's followed the series thus far. If this is your first time, I would love nothing more than for you to keep reading.

I am the author, Yuumikan.

Your support has allowed *I Don't Want to Get Hurt, so I'll Max Out My Defense* to successfully reach Volume 3.

I've tried to bring you the best book I could—once again, I would not be here without the help of so many others, so that is my way of returning the favor.

Between the second and third volumes, several important things happened.

First, they made a commercial.

I remember watching it and feeling like it was so unreal. I never dreamed anything like that would happen when I started writing, and I couldn't believe something so wonderful had actually come to pass.

That's a feeling I hope stays with me.

*   *   *

Second, there's going to be a manga adaptation. When I was told this, I was happy—and again, I could not believe my ears.

I can't draw at all myself, so seeing Maple's adventures take shape before my eyes is a source of constant joy.

There are a few more things I should say about this adaptation.

The *Bofuri* manga will be drawn by Jirou Oimoto.

He's got a cute art style that really conveys the charm of the characters and how much fun they have exploring together.

It'll be running in *Monthly Comp-Ace*, so I hope you'll pick it up when the time comes.

About the third novel—when I was writing it, I was clearly in a mood to jam in everything I like.

Reading back over it, that is far clearer to me than it was when I wrote it. I've added a number of extra descriptions and hopefully made it all easier to read.

I plan to continue taking things one task at a time, and I hope to bring you all more good news.

With that in mind, let me bring *I Don't Want to Get Hurt, so I'll Max Out My Defense*, Vol. 3 to a close.

Treasuring each step.

In hopes of more glad tidings.

And the prospect of a fourth volume in days to come.

Yuumikan